Hi, Charlotte,

Just a quick note ~~here~~ here in Indigo. L~~...~~ over the summer, but I'm not complaining ~~...~~ng a B and B has proved to be more fun than I expected.

The locals are planning a Cajun music festival for the fall, and they've enlisted my help. People want to raise money to revive the old opera house and promote tourism in the little town. The only one I know who's opposed is a woman named Joan Bateman. She moved here from the East about ten years ago and she's afraid an influx of tourists will ruin Indigo, but I think she's pretty much outnumbered. Besides, this place is so charming, with the bayou running through it and the old shotgun houses and opera house, it deserves a few visitors. I figure the money they spend will do more to keep the community alive than destroy it. Whoa, I'm starting to sound like a local myself. Maybe I've been here too long!

Send my love to Aunt Anne and your sisters, and especially my little cousin Daisy Rose.

Luc

Dear Reader,

I've only visited New Orleans once in my life. But I was immediately struck by the grace of the architecture and the passion of the people. From the music to the food to the clothing and art, everything about the city throbs with passion and a zest for life.

When I was offered an opportunity to participate in the Hotel Marchand continuity series, the sights and smells and sounds of Louisiana immediately returned to me. I took my characters through the historic architecture, let them indulge in the unique foods and stranded them in a pounding thunderstorm far up in the wilds of the bayou.

I had experienced a thunderstorm during my own trip. It stranded me with a group of friends in a quaint little restaurant next to a courtyard where the deluge clattered against wax-leaved, tropical plants. It was a glorious afternoon, and I learned then and there that Louisiana doesn't do a single thing in moderation.

New Orleans is a jewel. It is also tenacious and audacious. I know this great city, and the great state of Louisiana will be back, bolder and better than before.

I'd love to hear from readers with their own Louisiana stories, or from those who just want to say hi. You can reach me through my Web site at www.barbaradunlop.com.

Happy reading!

Barbara Dunlop

BARBARA DUNLOP
A Secret Life

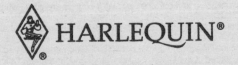

HARLEQUIN®

TORONTO • NEW YORK • LONDON
AMSTERDAM • PARIS • SYDNEY • HAMBURG
STOCKHOLM • ATHENS • TOKYO • MILAN • MADRID
PRAGUE • WARSAW • BUDAPEST • AUCKLAND

For Jane Graves, Kathryn Lye and Jennifer Green.
In honor of one memorable thunderstorm
in New Orleans.

ISBN-13: 978-0-373-38947-6
ISBN-10:   0-373-38947-7

A SECRET LIFE

Copyright © 2006 by Harlequin Books S.A.

Barbara Dunlop is acknowledged as the
author of this work.

www.eHarlequin.com

Printed in U.S.A.

Barbara Dunlop is the award-winning, bestselling author of thirteen books for Harlequin and Silhouette. She sold her first book to the Duets comedy line via cell phone while visiting the Smithsonian Air and Space Museum in Washington, D.C. During that same exhilarating trip, she won her second Golden Heart Award. Barbara now lives far up north in the Yukon Territory, where she is currently curled up in her log cabin working on her next story.

CHAPTER ONE

ANTHONY VERDUN knew he should feel guilty, but he hadn't felt anything but free since three o'clock Friday afternoon when he fired Clarista Phillips. He drew a deep, cleansing breath as his feet pounded the pathway between the pond and the artists' gate of Central Park on his Monday morning jog.

The woman was great with word processing and appointments, but her flirtatious manner had become embarrassing. Her fixation on Anthony had culminated in a pair of red lace panties in the interoffice mail, along with an explicit invitation involving peaches, whipped cream and silk scarves.

It wasn't that he had anything against silk scarves, or lace panties for that matter. But he was an old-fashioned guy. He preferred a little dinner, maybe even a drink before the first blatant proposition. He tapered his run to a jog as he exited the park, slowing for the traffic lights on Sixth Avenue, and finally switched to a walk.

His wet, khaki T-shirt clung to his skin in the warm, September breeze, while beads of sweat dampened his short, dark hair. He stretched his neck from side to side, listening to the vertebrae pop in relief as he crossed the street and headed for the Moulin Coffee

Bar. The bells on the door jingled against the rush hour traffic sounds, and the aroma of fresh coffee beans greeted him like an old friend.

He approached the counter, picking up a newspaper from the rack and stuffing it under his arm as he smiled at one of the regular counter clerks. "Large, black Colombian, please."

Young and pretty, with a tousled ponytail and bright red lips, she returned his smile as she rang in the purchase. The glint in her eyes invited conversation, but Anthony had a full day ahead of him. And after Friday's experience, he sure wasn't in the mood for ingenuous chitchat.

He pulled his cell phone from the hip pocket of his jogging shorts, pressing the speed dial for Kent Livingston's direct line. As he waited for the connection, he considered the bagels and sticky buns behind the glass case. He'd made time around the lake this morning, and he was in the mood to celebrate, so he pointed to the sticky bun and held up one finger.

Kent picked up on the first ring. "Livingston, here."

"Hey, Kent. It's Anthony."

"Anthony," Kent cooed in a singsong voice. "You sly son of a bitch."

"Huh?"

"Congratulations."

Anthony handed the clerk a twenty, trying to zero in on Kent's meaning. Had he heard about Clarista? If so, it was more than a little embarrassing. He sure hoped nobody else in the tight-knit New York literary world knew why he'd fired his assistant.

"Thanks," he muttered into the phone, dropping a couple of bills into the tip snifter and pocketing the rest of his change. He carefully balanced the coffee and the bun while working out an exit from the confusing conversation.

"Zane Randal's worried about the promotional copies making it to Berlin on time," he tried.

"Not a problem," Kent responded, his voice turning more serious as he shuffled some papers in the background. "I'll confirm with marketing this morning. Is Zane heading over on Friday?"

"Thursday," said Anthony, pushing open the coffee shop door with his elbow, giving up the buzz of conversation for the honks of Sixth Avenue. "His publicist set up a couple of radio spots and a reading."

"That's what we like to hear," said Kent. "The marketing rep will catch up with him on Saturday morning. He's at the Hilton?"

"He is," said Anthony, pleased that this pivotal leg of Zane's book tour was under control. As he paced up the sidewalk toward the Prism Literary Agency offices, he mentally clicked through the other priorities involving Kent.

"I'll have to call you this afternoon on the new Jules Burrell contract," he said. He was still waiting for a phone call from Joan to confirm the manuscript deadline.

Kent chortled. "Think I'll be passing that one up to Bo."

Anthony paused. They were passing Jules Burrell to Bo Reese? That didn't make sense. As the vice-president of author development, Bo was one of the top power-wielders at Pellegrin Publishing. He usually didn't bother with anything under seven figures.

"I figured you'd do that," Anthony bluffed, wondering if *Bayou Betrayal* might have hit a list. "I'll have to call you back."

He snapped the phone shut before Kent had a chance to realize Anthony had been caught off guard. Then he quickened his pace for the last two blocks, biting into his sugary breakfast and guzzling enough caffeine to jump-start his brain.

He nodded to the security guard in the lobby and took the elevator to twenty-two, where he said good morning to the receptionist at the Prism offices.

"Nice move, Anthony." Rosalind smiled and winked as he walked by, finishing off her greeting with a perky little salute.

Anthony didn't break his stride. Could Rosalind have heard about Clarista? Had somebody issued a memo or something?

He passed through his outer office, draining the coffee and tossing the paper cup into the trash. He'd take a quick shower before looking into the status of *Bayou Betrayal.* If the book had made a list, all kinds of things were possible.

"Verdun!" boomed Stephen Baker, bursting through the office door behind Anthony. "What a coup!"

Anthony swiveled to face his boss, hoping against hope this was a Jules Burrell matter and nothing to do with Clarista.

The barrel-chested, thick-necked Stephen slammed a copy of the newspaper on Anthony's oak desk. "*The New York Times* no less!"

Anthony quickly glanced at the newspaper. It was folded open to the front page of the lifestyles section. The name Jules Burrell jumped from the headline.

A write-up? A first page write-up?

Hot damn. A sizzle of excitement rushed up his spine.

He picked up the paper, trying not to look too surprised. But then he caught the name Joan Bateman in the opening paragraph, and his heart all but froze in his chest.

"No," he rasped, fists crumpling the flimsy pages.

Stephen clapped him on the shoulder. "Brilliant move. *Brilliant.*"

Anthony shook his head. "I didn't…"

Son of a bitch.

Joan Bateman was going to have him fired. No. Joan Bateman was going to have him killed. The only thing she'd asked in all these years was that Anthony protect her true identity.

Stephen pulled back in obvious surprise. "It wasn't you?"

Anthony's voice went up an undignified octave. "Of course it wasn't me."

Stephen hesitated. "Maybe it was Joan."

"Not a chance in hell." Then Anthony's brain suddenly engaged. *Clarista.* Clarista must have found a way to access the confidential files.

"I fired Clarista on Friday," he told Stephen, squeezing his eyes shut for a split second and pinching the bridge of his nose.

His boss raised a bushy eyebrow. "What for?"

"Inappropriate use of the interoffice mail."

"That's a firing offense?"

"It was on Friday." Anthony quickly scanned the rest of the article.

"And you think…"

"Of course I think. She swore up and down I'd regret it."

Stephen snorted. "Well, I don't regret it one little bit. The woman did us a favor."

"This is not a favor."

"Sales are skyrocketing."

"And Joan's going to fire me. In fact, Joan's going to fire the whole damn agency."

Stephen's expressive brows knit together. "You know you can't let that happen."

As if Anthony would be able to stop it.

"Anthony?"

"I don't control her, Stephen."

"Well, you'd better figure out how to control her. Get your ass to Indigo."

"So she can flip me off in person?"

"So you can put those good looks and charm to use."

Right. Stephen was really scraping the bottom of the barrel with that strategy.

He snapped the paper from Anthony's hands. "Don't think I don't see the admins panting after you."

"Nobody's panting after anybody." Well, except for Clarista. And Anthony didn't get the impression Clarista was particularly selective.

"Fix this," said Stephen, an edge coming into his voice. "Charm her. Flirt with her. Sleep with her, for all I care." His dark eyes turned to flints, and Anthony was instantly reminded that he was talking to the senior partner, and that Stephen hadn't got there by accident.

"This is one of those moments, Verdun." Stephen's voice was gruff with warning. "You can prove your worth to this firm, or you can make us a laughingstock."

Anthony swallowed. He got the message. He was going to Indigo, where he was to move heaven and earth to keep Joan in the fold.

AFTER TEN YEARS in Indigo, Louisiana, Joan Bateman was still considered a newcomer. Most days, that was a minor inconvenience. Today it was an out-and-out problem.

Back in Boston, she knew how to wield influence. She knew who was who and how to get to them. The Bateman family could call up a senator, sway a congressman or suggest when and where a newspaper editor should send a reporter.

But Indigo was different. She had no family here, no political connections. Cultivating influence, and doing it quickly, was her only hope of saving her beloved town.

Sitting at the dining room table in her neat little stilted Creole cottage, she puzzled over the guest list for Sunday's tea. The mayor, certainly, and perhaps the matriarch, Yvonne Valois.

Officially, everyone in town had expressed support for the plans to increase tourism. But Joan knew that couldn't possibly be true. Like her, others must be opposed to ruining the quiet serenity of Indigo. Her strategy was to quietly get to those who were opposed and give them the courage to speak up.

Trouble was, she had no idea who they were. Worse, she didn't know the interests or the histories of the town players, and what would motivate whom.

Her primary adversaries were obvious—Alain Boudreaux and Marjo Savoy. A strong supporter of the music festival, Alain was influential because of his deep family roots and his position as chief of the police department. Marjo, the funeral director, was head of the committee to restore the opera house—the centerpiece of the tourism push. The town had already agreed to fund emergency roof repairs to the building while they tried to get permission for a full restoration.

Joan tucked her shoulder-length hair behind her ears, as she laid out sheets of embossed card stock. Then she carefully opened her wooden box of calligraphy pens and stretched out her fingers to make them limber. She was going to do this right. A classy invitation to half a dozen influential people, salmon mousse, fine champagne, possibly caviar, then she'd pepper the event with subtle messages on the wisdom of keeping Indigo small and quiet—just the way it was.

That would be the beginning.

She opened a bottle of black ink, dipped her pen and began the lettering.

Halfway through addressing her first invitation, her telephone rang. She wasn't expecting any calls, so she let the machine pick it up while she kept working.

"Joan?" A familiar voice came over the speaker. "This is Heather."

Joan kept writing. She could call her sister back any old time.

Heather's tone rose half an octave. "You have to tell me if it's true."

Joan stilled the pen and glanced over her shoulder.

"And if it's true," Heather continued as the machine tape whirred, "tell me what you were *thinking*. Call me. Soon."

"What?" Joan voiced the question out loud.

For Heather to sound so rattled, it had to be something big.

Of course, big in Heather's world wasn't necessarily life-and-death in anyone else's. A catering mix-up or a fashion disaster could wait a few hours.

Joan went back to writing, but the phone rang again. It figured.

She finished the word *attendance,* wiped off her pen and rose from her chair, heading across the room as the greeting played.

She reached for the receiver.

"Joan?" came an unfamiliar, masculine voice.

She snapped her hand back.

"This is Alain Boudreaux."

Alain Boudreaux? The police chief had never called her at home before. Had he heard she was whipping up support against the music festival?

"I'd appreciate a call when you get this message."

As the machine clicked off, Joan's heart thunked. She quickly went over who she'd spoken to in the past week. She hadn't made a secret of not wanting to increase tourism. But she thought she'd been fairly circumspect.

Suddenly, there was a pounding at her front door.

She jumped.

Could it be Chief Boudreaux that quickly? Was he upset? Had he brought a posse? She debated whether to answer it, stay quiet or bail out the back way.

Whoever it was pounded again.

Curiosity got the better of her survival instincts, and she crept up to the small, beveled-glass window, squinting at the disjointed figure on her porch.

Anthony? What on earth was Anthony doing in Indigo?

"Joan?" he called, stepping back to gaze up at the white, two-story cottage.

"Anthony?" she called back.

He moved closer, squinting into the small window. "Let me in, Joan."

"What are you doing here?"

"I need to talk to you."

"About what?"

"Are you upset?"

"No." She wasn't upset. She was confused and getting a little jumpy. In fact, she was starting to hope this was all some kind of a bizarre dream.

He rattled the doorknob, and the catch gave way. No surprise in that; there weren't a lot of locks in Indigo. Just one of the things she was trying to protect by opposing the music festival and renovation of the opera house.

The painted door swung open to reveal the man who was her literary agent and lawyer. As always, the sight of Anthony took her breath away. Dressed in a very well-cut suit, he was an urbane, startlingly handsome man, with deep blue eyes, thick dark blond hair, a strong chin and a body that made women sit up and take notice.

And that wasn't simply her opinion. She knew other women took notice, because she'd watched them react to him for years. She also knew that Anthony knew. He had his pick. Always had, always would.

"What are you doing here?" She buried her inappropriate reaction down deep. "Did something go wrong with *Bayou?*"

The book had only been out a few days. It was a little too early to panic about numbers.

Anthony peered closely at her expression, crossing almost cautiously into her front hall and pushing the door closed behind him with a solid click. "Nothing's wrong with *Bayou.* Sales are going great."

"Good to hear."

His gaze strayed, and she followed it to the dining table.

"I was just addressing some invitations," she explained.

"I didn't mean to disturb you," he said.

She shook her head. "No problem. Can I get you—"

The phone rang yet again.

Anthony reflexively jerked toward it. "Don't answer that."

"I wasn't going to."

The greeting began.

Anthony crossed the room, then reached down and pulled the answering machine plug.

It took Joan a second to react. "What are you *doing?*"

"We have to talk."

She blinked. "About what?" Her theory that this was all a bizarre dream was quickly gaining credibility. She held still for a minute, waiting to wake up and start Tuesday all over again.

"Something's happened," said Anthony.

Joan closed her eyes and gave her head a little shake.

"Joan?"

She opened one eye. "You're still here."

He frowned.

She glanced down at her white, pleated blouse and linen slacks. "And I'm still here."

He took a step toward her, one hand tentatively reaching out. "Joan?"

She inhaled his spicy aftershave, wishing this really were a dream. What a perfect time to lean up and kiss him. She'd wondered about those full lips for years.

"We have to talk," he repeated.

"Okay." She nodded, shelving the dream theory for now. Surely if this was a dream, her subconscious would be making it a little sexier.

He looked way too serious. "Can we sit down?"

Maybe *Bayou* wasn't doing so well. Maybe he was going to drop her as a client. She'd heard the publishing business was downsizing, and authors were being let go all over the place.

"Just go ahead and tell me," she said, steeling herself.

He drew a deep breath and rubbed his chin. "It's like this…"

Joan waited, quickly growing impatient. "If it's bad news, it's bad news."

Whatever it was, she'd retain her composure. She'd draw on years of poise and practice learned at her mother's knee and keep her feelings bottled tight inside.

"There was a leak," he said.

She mentally shifted gears and glanced up at the ceiling. "Here?"

His shoulders dropped, and he shook his head. "Not that kind of leak."

"Oh."

"An information leak."

His point wasn't quite computing. "Information?"

He stepped closer. "Information about you." He paused. "Personally."

And then she got it.

It was like being struck with a lightning bolt. *"No,"* she rasped, shaking her head in denial as the breath hissed out of her body.

Heather's words screamed through her brain. "What were you *thinking?*"

At this moment, Joan didn't honestly know *what*

she'd been thinking. She'd put her faith in Anthony. She'd trusted him when he said he'd take care of her.

Now, she stared up at him, feeling as though she were seeing him for the very first time, wondering how he could have turned on her. "How could you—"

"Not *me*." A look of horror came over his face.

"Who else?" It couldn't have been anyone else.

He didn't answer.

"Who else knew?"

"There was a confidential file."

"You wrote it down?"

Blind trusts and numbered companies from here to Switzerland, and he wrote it down?

His eyes turned bleak, and he raked a hand through his hair. "Joan, I am so…"

She wanted to rant. She wanted to rave.

But she knew that wouldn't change a thing. All she could control now was how she reacted.

She called on every ounce of composure she could muster and compressed her lips. She had to think. There had to be something they could do, some way to salvage the situation.

"Who else knows?" she asked hoarsely. There was her sister, obviously. There was Anthony. There was the person with the confidential file and two lawyers in Atlanta.

Anthony glanced down at his feet and shifted.

"Who knows?" she repeated. She'd figure out exactly what they were dealing with, and they'd take steps to control the problem.

He glanced back up. And then he sighed. "The greater readership of *The New York Times*."

She staggered back. "It's…"

"In the paper. Yesterday."

Oh, no. No, no.

"And CNN picked it up this morning."

The room spun around her. "I think I'm going to throw up."

Anthony stepped forward, his hands closing around her shoulders. "Take a deep breath."

"That won't help." They'd still know. They'd all still know.

And it was her own fault. She'd grown complacent. After ten years, she thought she was home free. She thought the secret would stay locked forever behind the corporate screen Anthony had built.

So with *Bayou Betrayal,* she'd let loose. She cringed. "It has a *bondage* scene."

"Yeah, but that's the antagonist."

"My mother's going to read it. My *grandmother's* going to read it."

"It's fiction."

She started hyperventilating. "They'll think—"

"They'll think you're a creative and talented author."

"They'll think I'm a hack with loose morals."

"Who cares?"

"They're my *family.*"

"Then they should be proud of you."

Joan sagged. "It doesn't work that way."

"It's going to be fine."

"Not it's not." It might never be fine again.

"Joan." His voice sounded far away. "I know we can make this work."

After a second, his words registered.

Make it work?

Of course *he'd* make it work. Despite his show of

sympathy, he had to be elated by the turn of events. He'd been after her for years to do some publicity.

"You sure it wasn't you?" she asked.

He looked offended. *"Joan!"*

"It occurs to me that you have to be pretty happy about this."

"I'm not the least bit happy about this."

Did she believe him? Was she a fool to believe him? In the end, it didn't really matter. It was a done deal. Her family would shun her, and Anthony would head back to New York. And she'd be left here on her own.

All the more reason Indigo *had* to stay the same. She took another breath. She knew now how to mitigate the problem.

Crossing to the table, she sat down and picked up the calligraphy pen.

"Joan?" Anthony ventured from behind her.

"I'm a little busy right now." She drew a curved capital *P* with a flourish. "But thanks so much for stopping by."

He went silent.

She focused and finished the word *please.* "About the new manuscript," she said, dipping her pen. "I know it's a lot to ask, but could I have another couple of weeks to figure out the timing?"

Between books, she always did some spring cleaning, painted the shutters, wallpapered the den. There was something emotionally therapeutic about getting the clutter out of her life before she started a new project.

She was feeling extremely cluttered right now.

"Joan." Anthony shifted closer, his suit jacket swishing and his scent invading her space.

Her stomach tightened, but she ignored it. "I think it might be the music festival."

"The music festival?"

She nodded, still carefully forming letters. "It's taking up my mental space, and I really can't come up with a new story with all that going on."

The phone rang again, jangling through the cottage, making Joan's hand twitch a black streak over the page.

Anthony strode across the room and yanked the plug out of the wall. "I'm here to help."

"You know calligraphy?"

"You can't pretend this isn't happening."

"What isn't happening?"

"Your identity is out."

"Thank you *so* much for clarifying the situation. I really hadn't understood that from our conversation." She switched to a regular pen for the details.

He moved around the table, pulled out a chair and sat down. "We have to talk strategy. We have to make plans."

"I have a strategy."

"You do?"

"I'm addressing invitations."

His expression perked up. "A book launch?"

"A tea."

He paused. "Why?"

Joan moved a card aside to dry. "There are people here in Indigo who want to increase tourism."

Anthony didn't answer, but she could feel his tense questions.

"I think that's a bad idea," she continued. "And I'll tell you why. The beauty of living here is the peace and quiet, the sense of community, the slow pace of life and the opportunity for individualism. You bring in a bunch of gawking tourists, and that's all going to change in a heartbeat."

"So you're having a tea."

"Exactly."

"I'm not following your logic."

"That's because I'm an artist and you're a lawyer."

"I see."

He didn't see. He was being patronizing. The rat.

"I give a tea," she said, getting haughty right back at him. "I influence some pivotal people, turn the tide on this music festival, the opera house, the whole tourism thing, and Indigo stays exactly the same as it always was, protecting my lifestyle."

Her family would come around someday.

Maybe.

Then again, maybe not.

Anthony's voice turned patient. "And you don't think your fans coming to Indigo might have an impact on your lifestyle?"

"Why would my readers come to Indigo?"

Anthony was silent until she looked up.

"To see you, Joan." He looked completely serious.

But that was ridiculous. She wasn't a movie star. Nobody was coming to Indigo to see her.

Her problem was her parents and the bondage scene. Her pen slipped again. And these stupid invitations she kept ruining.

CHAPTER TWO

THERE WAS NO WAY in hell Anthony was letting Joan run around town to deliver tea invitations. She had to stay inside the house until they gauged the press's reaction to her identity. Not that he wouldn't make use of reporters. He just wanted to control the time and place.

"I'll deliver them for you," he said, reaching for the neat stack of envelopes in her hand. "Just give me the addresses." He wasn't wild about leaving her here alone, but it was the lesser of two evils.

She snapped them out of his reach and gestured to her front window. "Do you see a crowd forming out there? Do you?"

"That doesn't mean they're not in town."

Joan shook her head. "I'm going upstairs to change now. Then I'm delivering my invitations personally."

"Denial's not going to help," he told her.

"Neither is panic."

"I'm not panicking." He was taking logical, reasonable steps to ensure her safety and to keep control of the story. The last thing in the world he needed was for her to be accosted by an aggressive reporter or a local resident looking to make a few thousand dollars from the *National Inquisitor.*

"Getting changed now," she taunted over her shoulder as she headed for the staircase to the second floor.

"Barring the door now," he called back.

"You can't keep me prisoner." Her springy footsteps sounded on the hardwood steps.

"Watch me try."

He was glad she wasn't intimidated by the press. It showed self-confidence and spirit. Maybe she'd even agree to an interview.

He liked that idea. If they picked the right host and the right network, they could get out in front of this. Well-executed publicity would have a huge impact on sales. Pellegrin was already planning a second print run. There was a chance they could parlay it into a third and a fourth.

He pulled out his BlackBerry and did a quick check of the online bookstores. While he scrolled through some fine-looking numbers, there was a rap on the door.

Glancing at the staircase to make sure there was no sign of Joan, he tucked the BlackBerry into his pocket and headed for the small foyer.

He opened the door to a haughty blond woman wearing a pressed, pink linen suit, dangling earrings and an impressive diamond necklace against a perfect tan.

"Can I help you?" he asked, taking in her expensively streaked hair and precise makeup.

"Who are *you?*" she asked, tipping her chin and perusing him with blue eyes that catalogued, assessed, then dismissed.

"None of your business," he told her.

"Where's Joan?"

"Also none of your business."

She definitely wasn't a reporter, and he'd bet she wasn't local. A fan? Interesting demographic.

"Do I have to call the police?" she asked.

That surprised him. "Be my guest."

She didn't reach for a cell phone, so he was pretty sure it was a bluff.

"Joan?" she called into the cottage.

Anthony tried to push the door shut, but the woman thrust her hip inside, and he didn't have it in him to hurt her. He blocked the path with his body instead.

"Joan?" the woman called again. *"You all right?"*

Joan's quick footsteps sounded on the stairs. "Heather?"

"It's me," the woman called, shifting forward. "Who *is* this imbecile?"

"Anthony?" Joan rushed toward them. "What are you *doing?*"

"You know her?" he asked Joan.

"Of course I know her. She's my sister."

Anthony pulled back. "Your sister?"

The woman glared at him as if he was a blob of sidewalk gum. "Yes. I'm her sister."

Perfect. He supposed when a day took a downhill slide, it just kept right on going.

Heather brushed the front of her suit and straightened her sleeves, as if he'd somehow tainted her.

"This is Anthony Verdun," said Joan.

"You have a boyfriend?" Heather gave him another once-over, apparently coming to much the same conclusion as last time about his worth as a human being.

"He's my agent," said Joan.

"Like a lawyer?"

Anthony closed the door behind Heather, checking through the window to make sure nobody else was lurking in the hydrangeas.

"He is a lawyer. But he's a literary agent. He sells my books."

Heather looked him up and down. "So he's the one."

"Heather."

"I knew it'd be someone shady."

Anthony scoffed.

The woman kept her attention on Joan and waved her hand in the air. "How did he co-opt you into this nonsense?"

Joan's lips quirked into a half smile. "It's like a cult. He fed me bonbons and made me chant."

Anthony gave Joan points for her spunk, but Heather was starting to annoy him. "Did you forget the part where you say, 'Congratulations, Joan'?"

Heather arched a sculpted brow. "Congratulations? Puh-leeze."

"Your sister's about to hit a bestseller list."

"For pulp fiction."

Joan flinched, and Anthony clenched his jaw. He didn't care who Heather was, he wasn't about to stand here and let her insult his client. If she were a man, he'd have her up against the wall for that.

Instead, he jerked open the door. "I think you should leave now."

Heather's jaw worked in silence for a moment.

"I mean it," said Anthony.

"Why, you bloodsucking little upstart."

"*Stop,*" begged Joan, putting her fingertips against her temples. "I don't have time for this."

"I should think not," Heather huffed.

"I have tea invitations," said Joan.

"You are not leaving this house," said Anthony, snapping the door closed again.

Heather turned her attention back to Joan. "Just who the hell does he think he is?"

"My jailer, apparently," said Joan.

"I'm the guy who's turning this thing around."

Heather didn't even glance his way. "You want me to call the police? I could get Daddy—"

"Nobody's calling the police," said Joan. "Anthony's okay."

Okay? Well, wasn't that just…adequate.

He took a deep breath and warned himself not to let his emotions get mixed up in business. Joan's career was his priority, not his bruised ego. That meant he had to get this discussion back on an even keel.

"We need to sit down," he said to her. "And we need to talk about managing this issue."

"We need to talk about escaping to Europe," said Heather. "Mom and Daddy are—"

"Mom and Dad know?"

"They are literate," said Heather. "And even if they weren't, several of their friends have called."

Joan groaned and clutched at her stomach.

"You're not helping," Anthony said to Heather, moving toward Joan.

"*I'm* not helping? You're the one who got her into this in the first place."

"Yeah? Well maybe if she had a family who gave a damn about her feelings, she wouldn't have had to hide her career for ten years."

Heather let out a little squeak. "How dare you suggest we don't care about Joan."

"How dare you suggest I have motives other than her best interests."

"So you've represented her for free?"

Anthony didn't have a quick answer for that one. There was an answer, he just didn't have it at his fingertips.

Heather sniffed, putting her nose in the air and reaching for Joan's hands. "Go pack a few things. The jet's on the airstrip in St. Martinville."

"I'm not going to Europe," said Joan. "I'm going to deliver my tea invitations."

Anthony let out a long-suffering sigh. "Why do we have to keep having the same conversation?"

Joan gave him a sickly-sweet smile. "Because you keep getting it wrong."

He shifted closer still, capturing her green eyes in order to impress upon her the seriousness of the situation. "There could be reporters out there, lurking behind the cypress trees, waiting to pounce."

"You have delusions of grandeur," she said, staring right back.

"Your story was a section headline in *The New York Times*. I am not exaggerating the potential for publicity."

After a moment's silence, Heather spoke up. "I have to go with Anthony on this one."

Anthony glanced sideways at her and blinked. "Really?"

"Don't get me wrong. I'm still taking her to Europe."

"I'm standing right here," said Joan. "And nobody is taking me anywhere."

"That a girl," said Anthony. This was a moment in a million for an author. Joan needed to stay in the U.S., where she could capitalize on it.

"And I'm giving a tea." She turned to Heather. "You want to stay and make your crab puffs?"

"Joanie, we can be in Paris for breakfast."

"I'll deliver the damn invitations for you," said Anthony, whisking them out of Joan's hands. He could only fight on so many fronts at once, and Heather's Europe plan needed to be neutralized.

Once those invitations were out, he was willing to bet that Joan would stay put and host the party. He'd rather get her to New York, but Indigo was a lot better than Paris.

JOAN AND HEATHER watched Anthony's rented black sports car back down the dirt driveway and pull onto Amelie Lane.

"So, are you sleeping with him?" asked Heather as she let the cotton print curtains fall back into place.

"No, I'm not sleeping with him."

"Really?" Heather gave Joan the arched-brow, skeptical look that she'd perfected when they were growing up.

Joan felt a shiver of guilt, even though absolutely nothing was going on between her and Anthony. "He lives in New York. I hardly ever see him."

Heather shrugged beneath her Anne Klein blazer and tucked her bobbed hair behind one ear. "Too bad. If you ignore the attitude, he's pretty hot."

Joan wasn't about to disagree with that. Anthony was definitely hot. He also had an attitude.

"So, what did Mom and Dad say?" she asked, changing the subject to something only slightly more comfortable than her feelings for Anthony.

"That they were sure this was all some kind of a mistake."

Joan moved back from the window and into the

cluttered, brightly colored living room. "I'm sure they thought it was."

Heather took a cushioned rattan chair and crossed one toned leg over the other. The seat was Joan's favorite. Positioned beside a bank of windows, it overlooked the lawn, the cypress trees and the little pier that jutted out into Bayou Teche.

"What happened, Joanie? Last I heard you were writing history books."

Joan sat down on the floral print love seat opposite. "Brian died," she said softly, referring to her late husband.

Heather gave her a quizzical look.

"He was partway through a mystery novel," Joan said. "And then he died. I finished it in his memory." She smiled to herself. "And it was fun."

"So you made up a pen name."

"And I kept writing." Joan spread her hands. "And now this."

"What if you just denied it?"

"I'd be lying."

Her sister lifted a brow again as if to question the relevance of that statement. "Yeah?"

"Aside from the ethics of the situation, I'm pretty sure I'd get caught."

"Which makes me wonder…how did you keep it a secret this long?"

"A numbered company through Zurich."

Heather's dark red lips pursed in admiration. "Not bad."

"It was Anthony's idea."

"I bet Daddy could hide your tracks."

Oh, yeah, that was the answer. Engage her father in a conspiracy. "You thirsty?"

"Got a cosmopolitan?"

Joan stood. "Let me check." She drank more wine than martinis, but lime juice was a staple in Indigo, and she entertained often enough to keep a stocked bar.

Heather rose gracefully from her chair and followed. "I don't get what happened, Joanie."

Joan pulled the cranberry juice and lime out of the refrigerator, setting it on the breakfast bar that separated the dining area from the kitchen. "Mysteries are a lot more fun than history books."

"Did you want to be famous or something?"

"Of course not. I just wanted to have fun writing them. I figured, what's the harm? And I did hide it for ten years."

"See, that part blows me away. Ten *years*."

Joan scooped some ice from the freezer and dumped it into the martini shaker. "Something like that."

"So this wasn't your first book?"

"*Bayou* was my twelfth. And there's one more in line-editing."

Heather blinked at her in silence.

"What?" Joan asked.

"Daddy's going to freak."

Joan reached for the Absolut. "There was a chance he wouldn't freak over one book?"

"No. But now he'll freak even more."

Freak was probably the right word. Joan's stomach lurched again and, after a split-second hesitation, she poured some extra vodka into the shaker. "You want a double?"

"You bet." Heather perched herself on one of the high swivel chairs at the breakfast bar. She tapped her long, red fingernails against the Arborite. "I don't get why you had to publish them."

"Because that's what you do with novels."

"But why sell them at all? You don't need the money."

Not a bad question. Joan supposed she could have kept the manuscripts to herself. But it wouldn't have been the same. As much as she protected her privacy and solitude, she loved reading the reviews, and she got a big kick out of the reader comments that were sent to the unofficial Jules Burrell Web site. There was something satisfying in knowing a story she'd created spoke to people in so many different corners of the world.

"Joan?"

"It wouldn't have been the same," said Joan, capping the lid on the shaker.

"You bet it wouldn't have been the same." Heather gave a hollow laugh. "Hundreds of Daddy's friends and associates wouldn't have read your sweaty little saga and second-guessed his parenting skills."

Joan flinched. She hadn't meant to hurt her family. She knew the Batemans ranked popular fiction writing right up there with mud wrestling.

"Do you think he read it?" she asked, shaking the martinis.

Heather shook her head. "No."

"Did you read it?"

"When would I have read it? I called the jet right after reading the article this morning."

Joan poured the cosmopolitans into long-stemmed glasses, wondering if her family might be pleasantly surprised if they read her work. She realized that a big part of her was proud of her stories. "I could give you a copy. Are you curious at all?"

Heather stared contemplatively at her drink. "Quite frankly, I'm scared to death."

"Of what?"

"Of finding out that it's even worse than I thought."

Ouch.

"I'm at the Heidelberg Strings Friday night," Heather continued, oblivious to the fact that her insult had hit home. "With Jeffrey Plant. I don't want to have to explain your book to him and his mother."

Okay. Now that one definitely hurt. Joan contemplated her own drink for a long moment. "Yeah? Well, there's a bondage scene on page two-twenty-one. You might want to point that out to them."

Heather froze, glass halfway to her lips. "That's not even funny."

"It wasn't meant to be." Joan took a healthy swig. "Say hi to Monica Plant for me, will you?"

Heather's face blanched. A violinist herself, Heather considered her connections in the music community to be vitally important. "Have you completely lost your mind?"

Joan shrugged. She probably had. Her parents were going to kill her. And it wasn't as though she couldn't see their point.

Bayou Betrayal was a heart-pounding, action-packed, titillating read, aimed squarely at the mass market. It had little redeeming social value. It was simply a fun write and, hopefully, a fun read.

As Heather downed half of her own martini, there was a knock on the door.

Heather grabbed Joan's hand across the countertop. "You think we should hide?" she stage-whispered.

"It's probably Anthony," Joan whispered back.

"Would he knock?"

Joan put down her glass. "Of course he would

knock. I told you, we meet maybe once or twice a year." She headed for the door.

"I think you should be careful." Heather pattered behind her. "You've got enough problems without a news crew sticking a camera in your face."

Joan flashed her sister a look of disbelief. "News crew? You're starting to sound like Anthony." Still, she peeked through the beveled window before opening the door.

Not Anthony.

And not a news crew.

It was Samuel Kane, and Joan's stomach did a slow-motion slide to her toes. Samuel should have been the first person she thought of when her name went public.

In the past, she'd always been careful not to base her stories on real people or on real events. They all took place in Cajun country. And yes, the small town was similar to Indigo. But the stories themselves were pure fiction.

Until this one.

The murder-suicide of Samuel Kane's parents had formed the germ of her idea for *Bayou Betrayal*.

"Who is it?" Heather hissed from behind her.

Joan took a bracing breath and opened the door.

"Ms. Bateman?" Samuel Kane nodded, his tone low and melodious. He was a big, burly man with cropped black hair, deep-set eyes and a wide nose that looked as if it had been broken more than once. His skin was the color of burnished copper both from his hours in the sun as a carpenter and from his mixed heritage.

Joan sometimes saw him at church, and they'd certainly met around town, but they'd never engaged one another in conversation. There was only one reason for him to show up at her door today—he'd already read *Bayou Betrayal,* and she hadn't been nearly as vague as she'd hoped.

"Mr. Kane," she acknowledged, swallowing against a tight, dry throat.

"Who is it?" Heather demanded.

"I think you know why I'm here," he said.

Heather shouldered her way between Joan and the doorjamb. "Well, *I* don't know why you're here."

"Heather," Joan warned, stepping back, opening the door wider. "Please come in."

"You're letting him in?" Heather squeaked, glancing from one to the other.

"She's letting me in," said Samuel.

Heather looked him up and down. "You sure that's a good idea?"

Samuel perused Heather from head to toe. "You afraid I'll steal the silver?"

Heather crossed her arms over her chest and tipped up her chin. "I'm afraid you're a stringer for a tabloid."

Samuel's lip curled, and he gave Heather an insolent look few men would have dared. When she didn't flinch, he turned his attention to Joan. "I need to know if it's true."

"Please come in," Joan repeated.

"Joanie."

"Back off, Heather."

Heather's delicate nostrils flared for a second, but she stepped out of the way.

Samuel ambled through the doorway, ducking reflexively to accommodate his height.

Joan closed the door behind him.

"It's true," she admitted, bracing herself for his anger.

For a split second, his expression went blank. Then he blinked and drew back. "You have proof?"

"Proof?" What an odd question.

"Of my father's innocence."

Joan instantly understood, and her mouth formed a silent *oh*.

In her novel, Samuel's father didn't murder his wife and then commit suicide. In her novel, his father was framed by criminals who were after hundreds of thousands of dollars concealed in the walls of his house.

Samuel thought the entire book was true. And she'd unthinkingly given him false hope.

She swallowed past the lump in her throat. "I'm afraid the story is fictional."

Samuel's meaty hands slowly curled into fists.

"I made it up," she clarified, taking a step backward. Maybe Heather had been right about letting Samuel in.

Just then the front door opened, and Anthony strode into the hall. He stopped short, his eyes darting from one person to another. "What's going on here?"

Samuel ignored his arrival, pointing a finger in Joan's direction. "That book is about my parents."

"Whoa." Anthony stepped between Joan and Samuel. "We are not commenting on an accusation like that."

"It's true," said Joan.

"Joan," Anthony warned.

"The premise *was* based on his parents' deaths," she said, poking her head around Anthony's broad shoulders.

"*Joan,*" he rumbled between clenched teeth.

"But the story is fictional," she said.

Anthony gave a sharp nod. "There you go. The story is fictional."

"I'm really sorry," Joan said to Samuel, inching around to where she could see him again.

She'd love to be able to give him some peace of mind. Throughout the inquiry, she knew he'd insisted on his father's innocence. But nobody had listened to a teenager. And the evidence had been pretty compelling.

It was still pretty compelling.

She wished it wasn't.

"You didn't go over the inquiry?" asked Samuel. "The transcripts? You didn't piece together the police report and—"

"It's fiction," Anthony repeated.

Pain flashed through Samuel's brown eyes, but he blinked quickly, as if to banish it. "I thought—"

"You thought wrong," said Anthony.

"Stop," said Joan, putting a hand on Anthony's arm.

"He was innocent," Samuel insisted.

Joan didn't answer. There was nothing she could say or do to help the big man. She was a fiction author, not a criminal investigator.

Samuel glanced at all of them in turn, his voice dropping to a raw rasp. "He was *innocent.*"

"Maybe so," Joan lied softly.

Samuel's lips pursed and his eyes squinted down to slits of mistrust. He knew she was humoring him.

Then he squared his shoulders, glared once at Anthony and turned to walk out the door.

"Lawsuit," breathed Anthony as the door clicked shut.

"Tabloid," said Heather, ditching her martini glass and marching for the door.

CHAPTER THREE

ANTHONY WAS TOO GRATEFUL to finally have Joan alone to care what Heather might do or say to Samuel.

"That man will sue us for royalties," he said, pulling out his cell phone, searching his memory for the direct number of the Prism legal department.

"Then he'll win," Joan returned, gliding her fingers through her thick, brown hair as she moved toward the breakfast bar.

"I don't need you talking like that." Anthony gave up on his memory and punched in the number of the main receptionist.

Joan lifted her long-stemmed glass. "Talking like what?" She pivoted back toward him. "Oh, you mean telling the truth?"

"You don't get to decide the truth. A judge gets to decides the truth."

Joan scoffed at that and finished her martini. Then she promptly refilled it from the shaker.

"Whoa." Anthony snapped his phone shut and moved toward her. Though he could relate to the impulse, a drunk Joan would only make matters worse. "Slow it down there."

"It's weak," she said as he drew close. "The ice has melted."

"What is it?"

"A cosmopolitan."

"There's no such thing as a weak cosmopolitan."

She ignored him, draining a second drink. "You want one?"

"No, I don't want one." Well, actually he did. But he was exercising restraint.

She waved the empty glass in the air, walking around the end of the breakfast bar and into the kitchen.

"You shouldn't drink when you're upset," he pointed out.

"Why would I be upset? Just because you've trashed my reputation, ruined my family and probably got me kicked out of Indigo?"

"I've already told you I can fix it. If you'll just listen—"

"Don't you think you've done enough?" She popped the silver lid off the martini shaker.

"*I* wasn't the leak."

"Right." Her voice turned sing-song. "It was some mysterious mole with the *secret files.*" She poured in a few ounces of vodka and reached for the cranberry juice.

"The *confidential* files. Every business has to keep them."

"Whatever." She capped the shaker and swished it from side to side.

He rounded the breakfast bar and commandeered the shaker. "Getting drunk is not going to help."

"Who's getting drunk?"

He popped the lid with one thumb and dumped the martini mix down the sink.

"Hey!"

"Read my lips—"

"No, you read mine." She mouthed a pithy curse.

"I can't believe you just said that." Anthony had never imagined a word like that forming in Joan's brain, never mind coming out her mouth.

She reached for the shaker. "Believe it."

He snagged her wrist. "Oh no, you don't."

"Let go of me."

He didn't. "We need to focus here, Joan."

Her green eyes sparkled in the sunlight streaming through the window. "I am focused."

"Not on cosmopolitans."

"I was talking about the tea."

"Well, I'm focused on how Samuel is going to sue us."

She moved a little closer, her perfume wafting around him. "Done deal, Anthony. Samuel's already won."

"Because you'll feel compelled to confess to the judge."

"Exactly." She compressed her lips. "I tell the truth, the whole truth and nothing but the truth."

Anthony paused. "Say that again."

"Huh?"

He had an idea. It was a wonderfully simple, yet brilliant idea. "You're going to stand up and tell a judge *Bayou Betrayal* is based on an Indigo murder scandal?"

"Yes, I am."

Merry Christmas, Anthony.

His grip loosened on her wrist, and he had to fight himself to keep from turning it into a caress. This wasn't the time to think about her soft skin, the scent of her perfume, the sweet puff of her breath or the rounded curves beneath her tailored clothes.

He took a step back. "I know how we can skip the judge part."

"We write a big fat check?"

"You tell it all to Ned Callihan."

Her coral lips pursed, and for a split second he imagined kissing her. It was a fleeting, intense fantasy, where he pulled her flush against him and tasted that tender mouth for the very first time.

"From the News Network?"

Anthony nodded, tamping down his inappropriate reaction.

"How would that—" Her eyes went wide, and she took a step back. "Oh no, you don't."

"You tell the whole truth and nothing but the truth to Ned on camera. Five minutes. Then whiz, bang, we cut Samuel a check."

She shook her wrist out of his grip. "I can't believe you would suggest that."

"It would solve two problems."

"You have no soul."

While that was probably true, it didn't mean this wasn't a great idea. And he sure wasn't giving up on it without a fight.

HEATHER HAD NO IDEA where to find Samuel. His blue pickup truck had turned the corner of Cypress Street two minutes ago, but by the time she got there, he'd disappeared. There were no tire tracks, no dust, nothing.

She slowed her rented Audi to a crawl and checked out the parking lot of the general store and scanned the streets around the town lawn. Then, just when she was about to give up, she caught a glimpse of a blue tailgate. The truck was tucked beside the old Indigo opera house.

She shifted into second.

The man might run, but he couldn't hide from Heather Bateman. She followed the crescent around the town lawn, pulling into the opera house parking lot. She shut off the engine and set the park brake, exiting into the sharp sunshine and deep humidity of the Indigo afternoon.

The pillared front porch of the old building was covered with building materials and equipment—a circular saw, two-by-fours, a box of hand tools and bundles of cedar shakes. A machine chugged away on the gravel at the corner of the building, with a hose that wiggled all the way up the white siding. Loud, rhythmic cracks came from somewhere on the roof.

Looking up, Heather maneuvered carefully across the uneven gravel in her new Etienne Aigner heels. A leg came into view up on the gabled roof, and she recognized Samuel's faded blue jeans and leather, steel-toed boots. She stumbled but quickly righted herself as she moved from the parking lot onto the lawn.

"Samuel?" she called over the thwacking noise of the machine.

No response.

"*Samuel?*" she called a little louder, making her way to the bottom of the ladder that stretched up two and a half stories.

Nothing.

Either he couldn't hear her, or he was deliberately ignoring her. She had to admit, it was comforting to know he'd gone straight back to work. She had visions

of him heading for the nearest pay phone to make a deal
with a newspaper.

It was bad enough that her parents had to deal with
twelve—*twelve*—of Joan's novels coming to light. If
they had to cope with a salacious murder connection
on top of it, they'd faint dead away.

"Samuel!" she tried one more time.

Nothing.

Great.

She glanced from side to side across the emerald
lawn. There was nothing but houses and small businesses in the distance. She could try to find someone
to help—maybe that Anthony guy would climb up and
get Samuel for her. Or she could wait it out down here
in this steam room of a yard until Samuel was finished.

She glanced at her watch. Two o'clock. The man
could be up there for hours. Asking Anthony pain-in-the-
butt Verdun for help wasn't a particularly appealing
choice, either. Besides, he'd probably refuse just to spite
her.

Fine.

She took a deep breath and reached for the nearest
rung, reminding herself her family's honor was at stake.
The ladder was painted a cool, smooth gray, thank
goodness. Splinters would have added insult to injury.
She was careful not to damage her ruby manicure, and
she placed her shoes just so on each rung so that she
wouldn't break a heel or scuff a toe.

She glanced down once, blinking away vertigo, but
was happy to see there was still no one beneath her. It
wasn't the greatest day to be wearing a thong. But then
it *was* a hundred degrees out here.

Three more rungs.

Two more.

Finally, her head came up above the roofline.

Samuel had his back to her, about twenty feet away, up the pitch of the shake roof. He was on his hands and knees punching nails with a deafening air gun.

Heather climbed up two more rungs, then carefully maneuvered her leg around the side of the ladder, placing her knee on the rough shakes. Good thing she wasn't wearing stockings. She glanced at the surrounding buildings one more time. She was about to flash any Indigo residents within a hundred yards.

She put a hand on the rough roof, gritted her teeth, and inched her other leg around the ladder.

There. She'd done it.

She crawled a few feet from the edge, then stood up, straightening her clothes.

"Mr. Kane," she called between cracks of his nail gun. *"Samuel."*

He jerked his head around. "What the hell?"

She walked closer. "I need to talk to you."

He came to his feet. "We're nearly three stories up."

"I tried calling."

"Are you a lunatic?" With the advantage of the roof pitch, he had an awful lot of height on her. She was reminded all over again what a big man he was.

His faded blue jeans clung to his slim hips, but his chest and shoulders tapered out like a football player's. His biceps strained against his thin T-shirt sleeves, and the muscles of his chest were delineated against the damp fabric.

His face was attractive, in a rugged, dangerous kind of way that sent an unexpected shiver up Heather's spine.

"You shouldn't be up here," he growled.

Another shiver. "I need to talk to you."

"I'm off work at six."

Oh, no. She wasn't leaving him alone until six o'clock. She wanted this deal worked out before he had a chance to contact anyone else. "I need to know what you're going to do with your story."

His dark eyes narrowed, and his hands went to his hips. "I assume you're talking about my parents' murders?"

"Anthony seems to think there'll be a lot of publicity around Joan's book." Heather was hoping Anthony was wrong, but she couldn't afford to take any chances.

"So?" asked Samuel.

"So, I can see how a guy like you might be—"

"A guy like me?"

"Yes."

"What exactly am I like?"

She gestured to his clothes with her hand. "A…uh… working man."

He stared at her in silence, a grim tightness to his full lips. Chip on his shoulder or what?

She fluffed her sweaty hair, deciding to get right to the point. "I'm prepared to make you an offer."

His brows went up.

"Ten thousand dollars." She hoped that was enough. Surely ten thousand dollars was a lot to a carpenter in Indigo, Louisiana.

"For?"

He hadn't struck her as slow.

"Keeping this whole business to yourself, of course."

He laughed then. It was a deep chuckle of disbelief

that rumbled through his broad chest but definitely didn't meet his eyes.

Damn. She'd insulted him. "Twenty thousand?"

"To keep my mouth shut?"

"I'm sure you can see—"

"What gave you the impression I could be bribed?"

Anybody could be bribed. "It's not a bribe."

"The hell it's not."

"Thirty thousand."

"Get off my roof."

"Forty?"

He gave her an insulting once-over from her breasts to her toes and back again. "Listen, lady. I talk to who I want, when I want. And no spoiled brat's checkbook is going to change that."

Spoiled *brat?* She drew herself up to her full five foot four and crossed her arms over her chest. "There's no need to get insulting."

"You started it."

"I'm not insulting you."

"You just offered me forty thousand dollars in hush money."

"You don't want forty thousand dollars?"

"I'm not for sale."

"Listen, you—" Heather just barely stopped herself from delivering the scathing retort. Joanie was what mattered here, Joanie and the Bateman reputation. She swallowed her pride and reframed her offer. "In consideration of the money you could likely make selling your story to the media, I'm prepared—"

Samuel took a step closer, peering down at her. "What have I ever said or done that would lead you to believe I'd sell my parents' *murders* to the highest bidder?"

Heather opened her mouth. Was he saying he wouldn't go to the media? Was he insulted because she'd suggested he would? She searched his expression, trying to decide if this was about a moral code or upping the ante.

"You're not going to tell your story?"

"That's none of your business."

"So you *are* going to sell the story." Just how high was she going to have to go?

His expression flickered no more than a millimeter. "I'm going to throw you off this roof in a minute."

Heather felt a reluctant smile forming on her lips. "Well, that is one way to solve your problem."

His brown eyes glinted ever so slightly. "Isn't it, though?"

"I could write you a check right now."

"Goodbye…"

"Heather."

"Goodbye, Heather."

"I can't leave."

"Sure you can."

She shook her head. "Not without your assurances that you're not going to hurt my sister."

He stared at her in silence. "My word good enough?"

Heather hesitated. "You tell me."

He paused and seemed to think for a moment. "I'm not interested in money. But if I have a chance to prove my father's innocence, I don't care who I hurt."

"If you want to hurt Joan, you'll have to go through me."

Samuel's sharp nod told Heather he was confident he'd prevail. And, though she hated to admit it, she had a feeling he was right. She might have money and power on her side, but there was something about Samuel that intimidated the hell out of her. He wasn't a man she'd want to cross.

"Fair enough," said Heather. Joan had made it pretty clear her novel didn't contain new evidence that would help Samuel. And if he was after money, he'd have been wise to say yes to the forty thousand.

Heather turned to go. But as she focused on the lawn below them, she experienced a sudden, overpowering wave of vertigo. She steeled herself and took a step forward anyway. She wasn't afraid of heights. And they weren't that far off the ground. She and Joan had had a tree fort when they were kids. Ladders were nothing.

She kept going.

Five more steps and she was at the edge of the roof, her trepidation rising by the second. She could do this. She *would* do this. She'd climbed up that ladder, and she'd climb back down again. She gripped one of the rails, and the ladder shifted along the gutter.

Everything inside her froze.

Samuel swore behind her, and she heard his footsteps on the cedar shakes.

"It's easy," he rumbled.

"I know." She took another baby step. "I'm fine." She put her hand gingerly on the top rung. She'd slide her leg around, just like she'd done when she got off.

She glanced at the ground, and it swayed crazily to one side.

"You're shaking," said Samuel.

"I am not."

He sighed, and moved up beside her. "I'll hold it steady."

"There's no need." Her voice came out raspy against her dry throat.

He pointed. "Grab right here."

She did.

"Now put your leg on the rung."

She tried to move her foot, she really did. But for some reason, it was frozen to the roof.

"How the hell did you get up here?" Samuel muttered.

Heather didn't answer. She was afraid it would come out as a whimper. Maybe she could make a call. Maybe they'd come and get her by helicopter.

"You okay?" asked Samuel.

"Fine," she breathed.

"You afraid of heights?"

"No."

"You going to get on that ladder?"

She didn't answer.

"Heather?"

"What?"

"Just how scared are you?"

She tightened her grip on the ladder and inched herself forward, refusing to let him know she was nearly paralyzed. Careful not to look down, she hooked a toe on the gutter and transferred her weight.

The gutter started to give way, and she shrieked.

Samuel's arm was around her in a split second, yanking her back against his body. "Damn," he muttered above her head.

"I'm fine," she insisted, but her voice was shaking.

He loosened his grip. "Don't move."

"Okay." That one she could do.

He slowly let her go. Then he effortlessly swung

himself out onto the ladder and backed down a couple of rungs. He let go of the ladder with one arm and held his hand out to the side, making a space for her.

"Hang on to the top of the ladder and step around on this side," he said. "If anything goes wrong, I'll grab you."

Heather nodded, swallowing as she assessed the situation.

"Do not look down," he warned.

She nodded again. It didn't seem nearly as scary with Samuel's big body between her and death.

His voice went softer. "Piece of cake."

She took a step.

"Grab on right there," he coaxed. "And turn around."

She did, and the ladder felt solid beneath her hand. She breathed in, daring to move backward toward the edge. It was stupid, but now she couldn't help thinking about his angle and her thong. "Can I trust you to be a gentleman?" she asked.

"Not even a little bit."

She shot him a glare over her shoulder.

"If I have to grab you, I have to grab you. I'm not gonna be careful about the target."

"I wasn't..." *Oh.*

"What?"

She studied his expression. "Forget it." She faced the roof again. Nothing to do but get this over with.

With both hands on the top rung, she inched her toe onto the ladder. When one foot was solid, she moved the other, breathing a sigh of relief when Samuel's arm locked her in.

"You actually thought I would check out your underwear?" he rumbled.

"It had crossed my mind," she confessed.

He moved down a rung and waited for her. "What the hell kind of men do you hang out with?"

She carefully stepped down, her muscles clenched, her damp palms inching along the painted rails. "There's nothing wrong with the men I hang out with."

He moved again. "There is if they're all looking up your skirt."

"They don't look up my skirt." At least not without an invitation.

"Then why did you think I would?"

"It was an overreaction, okay?"

"First, you try to bribe me," he grumbled. "And then you accuse me of being a Peeping Tom."

Heather took another rung. "Get over it, will you? How was I supposed to know you were a paragon of morali—" Her foot slipped. Her heart went to her throat.

His arm closed tight around her waist, and he was a solid wall behind her. "You're fine. I've got you."

"Damn," she muttered, adrenaline thrumming through her body.

"You okay?" he asked.

She nodded, searching for the rung with her foot.

He didn't immediately let her go. Which was perfectly okay with her. If she had to stumble on a ladder twenty feet off the ground, Samuel was definitely the guy she wanted hanging on to her.

His broad palm was splayed across her stomach, and his solid abs were pressed against her rear end.

"I'm not much of a paragon at the moment," he said.

"You just saved my life."

"Yeah. But now you've got me thinking about your underwear."

CHAPTER FOUR

"JOANIE?" Heather's voice hissed in Joan's ear as the bedsprings sagged beneath her weight.

"What?" Joan groaned, refusing to open her eyes. Maybe sending the jet back and letting Heather stay a few days had been a bad idea. It felt as if she'd only been asleep for a few minutes.

"I hear something." Heather slipped under the covers in the queen-size bed.

"Those are frogs," said Joan, wrapping her arms around her pillow and burrowing her face more deeply into its softness.

"Not the frogs. The thumping noise."

"Those are the cypress trees."

"It's not trees."

"Yes, it is."

"Joanie."

"Do you *still* get nervous in the dark."

"I don't get nervous in the dark."

"You're nervous now."

"That's because of the thumping noise."

"There is no thumping—"

Something whapped against the side of the house.

"That," shrieked Heather, scooting closer on the bed.

Joan opened her eyes, blinking in the dim bedroom.

Moonlight wafted through the opaque curtains and danced along the ceiling and the walls.

"What on earth?"

"Call the police," Heather hissed, fumbling for the phone on the bedside table.

Joan slipped out of bed.

"Where are you going?"

"To look out the window. It's probably an alligator." They didn't often come this close to the house, but every once in a while...

"What if it sees you?"

"We're on the second floor."

"So what?"

Joan pulled back the curtain, squinting into the yard. "They can't jump."

"Can you see it?"

"No."

"Then how do you know it's not a person?"

"Because Indigo is one of the safest places in the country. We don't even lock our doors."

"You didn't lock your door?"

There was another thump, then a scraping noise.

Joan had to admit it didn't really sound like an alligator anymore.

"I'm dialing 911," said Heather.

"Don't call the police." Joan crossed the room and whisked the phone from Heather's hand.

She was still avoiding Alain Boudreaux. She hadn't returned his call. And she didn't want to have to defend her position on the music festival.

"We're just going to sit here and let ourselves get attacked."

"There's no crime in Indigo."

There was another thump, then a creaking noise.

Heather's voice went shrill. "Then what's that?"

"Probably a reporter." Now that the words were out, Joan realized it was a distinct possibility.

"Then call Anthony."

Joan glanced at the clock. "I'm not calling Anthony at three in the morning."

"Then I'm calling the police."

"I'm sure whoever it is will go away," said Joan. Maybe they just wanted pictures of her house. Surely they didn't expect an interview at this hour.

"Before or after they discover your doors are unlocked."

Joan hesitated. Heather did have a point. Reporter or not, she didn't like the idea of somebody meandering into her house at night. Maybe Anthony could drive by and scare them off.

She took a breath. "Okay. I'll call Anthony at the B and B."

"Tell him to bring a gun."

Joan dialed Anthony's cell number. "He's not bringing a gun."

"A knife? Mace?"

The ringing tone sounded in Joan's ear. "I'll just tell him to drive by. The lights should scare off any reporters."

"What if something goes wrong?"

Joan wished her sister would calm down. Nothing was going to go wrong. There was an overzealous reporter tromping through the hydrangeas, that was all. Heather had lived in a big city way too long.

"Verdun here," came Anthony's groggy voice.

"Anthony? It's Joan."

"Joan? What's—"

"Heather hears a noise."

"You hear it, too," said Heather.

"What kind of a noise?" Anthony sounded more awake, and there was a rustling in the background.

"Thumping, creaking. I thought it was an alligator—"

"What is it?" It sounded as if he was moving around.

"A reporter, maybe?"

"There's a *person* in your house?"

"Not in my house. On the porch. Maybe. I think…" She shouldn't have called Anthony. She should have checked the porch herself. Heather was making her jumpy.

"I'll be right there."

"I was thinking you could just drive by—"

"I'll be right there."

"There's no need to—"

The phone went dead.

"What's he doing?" asked Heather.

"He's on his way."

Another thump sounded, louder this time. Even Joan flinched.

Heather moved to the middle of the bed. "I sure hope he brings a gun."

ANTHONY ARRIVED within minutes. As his headlights flashed against the side of the house, there was a distinct sound of footsteps running down the back stairs.

Joan rushed to the window and stared across the lawn toward Bayou Teche, trying to make out a figure running through the trees. But it was too dark to see anything but shadows. It could have been a man, could have been a woman, could have been a dog for that matter.

Anthony pounded on the door, then pushed it open as Joan dashed down the stairs.

"Did he break in?" he asked, as she rounded the breakfast bar and hit a light switch above the sink.

The low light illuminated Anthony's face as Joan shook her head.

"They ran when they saw you coming," she told him.

"Your door was unlocked."

"It's always unlocked."

He frowned. "What do you mean?"

Joan gestured toward the front door. "The lock doesn't work. I never—"

"You're kidding." Anthony turned back to examine the catch. He clicked it a few times with his thumb. "Why the hell didn't you get it fixed?"

"There was never any reason—"

"Security. Privacy. *Safety*. Those aren't reasons?"

She resented the censure in his tone. "Indigo is a perfectly safe community."

Heather appeared in the kitchen, holding a silk robe closed over her nightgown. It reminded Joan that she was standing in front of Anthony in her short, peach nightgown—and the light was streaming in from behind her. She shifted to one side.

"Tell me everything that happened," Anthony demanded as he returned to the front door and pushed it shut.

His faded T-shirt and thin, gray sweatpants molded to his athletic body. The shirt was wrinkled, and Joan wondered if he'd slept in it. Or maybe he'd just thrown on the outfit for the drive over. Or maybe she should stop speculating.

No. That wasn't about to happen.

He looked different somehow. It was more than just the casual clothes; there was something unguarded, almost rugged about him. His chin was shadowed with dark stubble, and his usually perfect hair was mussed. Not to mention the way the T-shirt delineated well-developed arm and shoulder muscles. Anthony was a lot sexier under his pressed suits than she'd ever imagined.

And that was saying something.

"I heard a noise," said Heather. "I woke Joan up. She told me it was frogs."

Anthony raised his eyebrows. "Frogs?"

"They can get pretty loud at night," Joan defended.

"Somebody was trying to break in," said Heather.

"We don't know that," said Joan. "Heather's a nervous sleeper. They were probably just—"

"Prowling around on your porch?" Heather moved in closer, her body forming shadows against the small kitchen light.

"It might have been a reporter," said Joan, trying to stay logical—and concentrate on keeping her gaze above Anthony's neck. The room was getting hotter, and her skin was growing sensitive beneath the satin of her nightgown.

"Might have been," he agreed with a nod.

It took Joan a second to recapture the thread of the conversation.

Anthony raked his messy hair back from his forehead with spread fingers.

She controlled a little shudder of reaction.

"Okay," he said. "We're not going to figure out much tonight. You two go to bed. I'll camp out on the couch."

Joan blinked. Oh, yeah. That was a great idea. A sexy, tousled Anthony in her house overnight? She didn't think so. "You're not staying."

"Of course I'm staying."

Her chest contracted, inner thighs tingling. "Whoever it was is halfway down the bayou."

"They might come back."

"Yes, they might," Heather agreed. "You have a gun?" she asked Anthony.

Anthony shook his head. "Afraid not."

"We don't need a gun," said Joan. And they didn't need a bodyguard, especially one that tempted Joan to do something really embarrassing. "We'll block the front door with a chair or something, and I think the back lock still works."

Anthony and Heather both stared at her in silence.

She glanced from one to the other. "What?"

"You actually think there's a chance in hell I'd leave?" Anthony's jaw went hard and his lips compressed.

"Of course." But Joan's voice faltered. He didn't look like a guy who was leaving anytime soon.

He moved forward. "Take off and just leave you to fend for yourself?"

Okay. This was getting silly. Joan rolled her eyes toward the ceiling. "I've been fending for myself for ten years now."

Something flickered in Anthony's expression, but she couldn't quite place it.

"Well, I'm going to bed," said Heather. "I feel a lot

better knowing Anthony is here." With a toss of her blond hair, she turned and headed up the stairs.

"See that?" said Anthony. "Even Heather admits I should stay."

"Heather's sleeping in the guest room," said Joan, trying to turn his attention to the practicalities of the situation. "And my couch is way too small for you."

It was ridiculous for him to sleep in her cottage just because something went bump in the night.

"I'll sleep on the floor," he said.

"You're not going to sleep on the floor."

He moved closer still, and his blue eyes darkened for a split second, making her shiver with awareness.

"Where would you suggest I sleep?" he asked softly. If it was anybody but Anthony, Joan would have interpreted the words as innuendo.

"In your bed. At Luc's B and B."

"Not going to happen."

"Anthony."

"What?"

"I can't let you do this."

They stared at each other. It was a test of wills, and the air crackled between them.

A small smile grew on his face. "You, my dear, have no choice." He crossed to her wicker couch.

"It's my house."

"And I'm your lawyer."

"You're my agent."

He shrugged. "Same difference." He tested the floral patterned cushions with the flat of his hands. "Besides. I don't see how you're going to stop me."

This was ridiculous. He was a good foot longer than the narrow couch. She approached him, folding her arms over her chest. "Fine. You take my bed. I'll take the couch."

He straightened. "Yeah. Right."

She tipped her head, all but falling into his slumberous eyes. Their gazes caught and held. They were both silent as the bayou croaking rose around them and the tree branches creaked in the yard.

His tousled hair made him more approachable than usual. His shadowed face and the dim light played tricks on her senses. His musky scent wafted around her, and his lips parted ever so slightly, ever so invitingly.

She swallowed.

"You don't get it, do you, Joan?" he rumbled, and she wished he would reach out and touch her. A brush with those hands, on her face, on her shoulder, on her breasts.

She swayed a little. "Get what?"

"They go through *me* to get to you, not the other way around."

He looked down at her peach nightgown, and his blue eyes turned to a midnight sky. Her muscles tensed and her skin tingled as he made his way from her breasts to her stomach to her bare legs.

What would happen if she touched him?

What would happen if she kissed him?

While her imagination tested the sensations, his hand rose. His fingertips brushed her hair back. The touch on her skin was light, insubstantial, but it ricocheted through her, igniting sensations in every corner of her body.

She covered his hand with hers, pressing it against her cheek, wishing, yearning, wondering how she'd gone so long without discovering…

Their eyes locked.

She waited. But he didn't lean forward, didn't close the gap. As the seconds ticked by, she wondered if she'd misinterpreted his touch. She loosened her hand, suddenly embarrassed.

Anthony interested in her?

The idea seemed ridiculously far-fetched.

She drew away, adopting a matter-of-fact tone. "I don't think they'll be back."

He let his hand fall to his side. "You're probably right."

"Is there any point in me asking you to leave?"

He shook his head.

She took another step back. "Then I'll get you a pillow and blanket."

She turned and ducked her head, unwilling to meet his eyes again. She'd obviously misread the signs. She was just another woman to him. Just another in a long line of those who found themselves attracted to his good looks and lazy charm.

She opened the linen closet and extracted a plump pillow and a cream-colored quilt. Good to know up front. Embarrassing, but not as bad as if she'd become a notch on his bedpost.

ANTHONY'S CHANCE at sleeping was shot. Even if his legs hadn't hung over the arm of the narrow couch, his acute arousal and his memories of Joan's smoky jade eyes would have done him in for the night.

He'd thought from the first second he met her that she was a gracious, attractive and highly sensual woman. Of course, he'd ruthlessly squelched that reaction, since she was married at the time.

Then she was newly widowed. And after that, she was a valued client. She was still a valued client, and he had absolutely no business lusting after her—even if it was the middle of the night, even if she did look like a tousled goddess in that short little lacy number, and even if her eyes sent messages straight to his heart, all but begging him to pull her into his arms and kiss her until time stood still.

He couldn't kiss her. He couldn't touch her. He couldn't even *think* about kissing her or touching her.

He was here to take care of her, to see her through this crisis and make sure it didn't ruin her career.

He punched the pillow and shifted his cramped legs on the little torture chamber of a sofa. He had to figure out how to get her in front of an interviewer of *his* choice, not some bozo who was willing to camp out on her porch. If he handled this situation properly, he was sure he could boost her career and for the most part keep her privacy intact.

Shortly after six, footsteps sounded on the ceiling above him. He assumed it was Joan, since Heather didn't strike him as an early riser. He pushed into a sitting position and shook off the vestiges of fatigue and frustration. He'd managed on less sleep than this, and he could keep his lust in check when necessary.

NORMALLY, Anthony wasn't bothered much by guilt, particularly when he knew the end would justify the means. So when Joan announced she had a hair appointment that morning, he shamelessly thought up all the ways to use it to his advantage.

First, he was more than happy to move her out of Indigo and into the anonymity of Lafayette. And secondly, Lafayette was the home of a small network affiliate, giving him his first realistic interview possibility.

He convinced Joan and Heather to get full make-overs and manicures at the salon by offering to pick up the tab. His plan might not ultimately work, but having a camera-ready Joan within a few miles of a television studio definitely gave him a running start.

He was sitting on a soft, cream-colored leather sofa in the waiting room of Très Jolie, downing complimentary coffee while waiting patiently to get through to the news director at KCLA. He was sure he'd get better service if he mentioned Joan's name, but he didn't want to get specific with anyone but the top decision-maker.

There was a local newspaper on the coffee table in front of him, and he'd already found a page three article on Joan. It had a picture, but it was an older one, and he didn't think any of the salon employees or patrons realized who she was, particularly considering her face was bare of makeup and her hair was a mass of foil paper and gelatinous liquid.

She caught his eye, and he shot her a smile. He was happy to see her looking relaxed for the first time since he'd arrived.

"Raymond Miller here," came a voice on the other end of Anthony's cell phone.

Anthony turned away from Joan. "Mr. Miller. This is Anthony Verdun."

"So my assistant informed me."

"Thank you for taking the time to talk to me. I'm with the Prism Literary Agency in New York City."

"Is this a joke?"

"This is not a joke. I represent Joan Bateman. She writes as—"

"I know who Joan Bateman is. I've left three messages at your office."

"I'm in Lafayette at the moment."

"Really?" The man's tone changed. "Call me Ray."

Anthony smiled. "Before we go any further, Ray, are you able to set up a live network feed?"

"Are you offering me an interview with Joan Bateman?"

"Let's just say I'm exploring my options."

"You have a competing offer?"

"It's not about money."

"Okay."

"Can you do the live feed?"

"Absolutely. Hang on." The sound went muffled for a second. "Sorry about that."

"No problem," said Anthony. "I'll be honest with you, Ray. Joan is shy, and I'm not sure I'll get the go ahead today."

Ray chuckled. "I'm more than willing to set it up on spec."

"Great. I want a female interviewer. Low-key, nobody aggressive. I'll be right there with Joan and I'll shut it down in a heartbeat."

The sound went muffled at Ray's end again. "We can feed in Charlotte Newcastle from L.A."

Anthony shook his head. "I want somebody in the studio with Joan."

Ray drew a breath. "Well, that presents—"

"Take it or leave it." Anthony was going for intimate and low-key, not high-tech flash. Charlotte Newcastle would probably intimidate the hell out of Joan.

"The only female interviewer I can give you in person is Karen St. Claire. She does cooking and local human interest."

"I'll need to meet her." Anthony could live with a

human interest reporter. He glanced back at Joan and Heather. Hopefully, they'd take another couple of hours.

"I'll set it up."

"I can be there in half an hour."

"Does this mean it's a go?"

"This means I'll meet Karen. If the setup looks right, I'll present the offer to Joan."

"Do we need to talk money?"

"Money's not the issue."

"What is the issue?"

"Joan Bateman's comfort level."

Ray paused. "You'll like Karen. Joan will like Karen."

"We'll see. Thank you, Ray." Anthony flipped his phone shut.

As he tucked it into his pocket, he caught Heather's quizzical gaze. She was definitely going to fight him tooth and nail on this.

Maybe he could bribe the esthetician to give her a massage—or maybe put her in a mud pack for a couple of hours. Yeah. That would work.

He rose from the couch, tossing Heather a benign smile as he headed for the reception counter.

CHAPTER FIVE

JOAN FELT fantastic.

It had been way too long since her last haircut, and the stylist had done something new this time. She'd textured Joan's hair so that it was light, sleek and shoulder-length. Then she'd added auburn highlights that caught the sunshine as Joan twirled in front of the three-way mirror in DKNY's boutique.

The wide pleats in her short, cream-colored skirt lifted ever so slightly. She tucked in the tags of a contrasting mauve silk blouse and adjusted the collar on a jewel-speckled jacket that matched the skirt.

"I'm just saying that if you ignore it, it'll only escalate," said Anthony. His tone was relaxed, but he obviously wasn't enjoying her impromptu fashion show. His fingers were tight on the arms of the chair.

Heather's mud wrap was going to take another hour or two and, unlike Anthony, Joan was happy to kill time in the boutique.

"The interest is going to die down on its own," she said with complete conviction. It wasn't as if she were a movie star. Sure, maybe there was a novelty factor in discovering the identity of a mystery writer, but it was a fifteen-minute thing.

"The interest is going to heat up."

"You're nuts."

"Maybe. But I've been at this for a lot of years. I want you to think logically for a minute."

She glanced down at her open-toed sandals. "You think pumps would look better." That was logical as far as she was concerned.

"It's the forbidden fruit syndrome."

She glanced up. "What forbidden fruit? I'm allowed to buy pumps if I want them."

Anthony gave a frustrated sigh and shook his head.

She sashayed toward him, passing a potted fern that screened the dressing area from the rest of the store. Soft music wafted down from ceiling speakers, muting the conversation of the other shoppers.

"I get it. You're saying *I'm* the forbidden fruit." She was feeling brave enough to be flirtatious today. He was back to his safe old self—clean shaven, well-pressed and ambitious. She could handle him like this.

But then his eyes darkened, and she caught a glimpse of the man he was last night.

"You are definitely the forbidden fruit in this scenario," he said.

His tone should have made her uncomfortable, but she couldn't muster up anything but satisfaction. At least he wasn't completely oblivious to her as a woman. She wished she'd tried on a sexier outfit. Maybe she'd go for that black sequined dress next.

"Truth is, the longer you hide, the more appealing you become."

She wanted to ask him if she was becoming appealing to him, but that would be over the line. Theirs was a professional relationship. She'd be foolish to play with the boundaries.

"One little interview," he continued. "And then they'll leave you alone."

Joan gestured around the store. "They *are* leaving me alone. You see a crowd? You see a camera? That person on my porch last night was probably nothing more than a common thief."

And she still had her family to think about. She'd have to call her parents soon, and she'd rather call to tell them she was lying low than call to tell them she was doing an interview. She wasn't the only one caught up in this predicament.

"You're delightful. You know that?"

She gauged Anthony's expression but couldn't tell what he was getting at. "Why, thank you," she ventured.

His voice dropped a notch. "And you're beautiful."

A small shiver ran through her. Were they going to play with the funny flirty thing again?

He rose from his chair, and she took a step back. "You'd be a natural on camera."

Okay. There it was. She shook her head. "You think you're so suave."

He took another step forward, determination in his stride, in his expression and in the set of his shoulders. "There's this local reporter."

"No."

"Her name is Karen St. Claire."

"Not a chance."

"She does cooking reports. I met her. She's—"

"You *met* her? When?"

"While you were getting highlights."

Joan couldn't believe it. While she had been relaxing in the salon, Anthony had been out on media recon. Did the man never slow down?

"They can give us a live feed to the network, and—"

"*Live?*" she squeaked. She'd assumed he was talking about a newspaper reporter.

A sales clerk approached in Joan's peripheral vision. "How do you like the jacket?"

Anthony pulled out his credit card and handed it to the woman without taking his eyes off Joan. "We'll take the whole outfit. You want pumps?"

"No, I do not want pumps." Who said she wanted the outfit, either? Although it was a great outfit.

"Okay," he said easily.

Joan waited until the woman left. "You are out of your mind."

"You look fabulous."

"Nice try."

He was conning her, she knew. But there was something about Anthony saying she looked fabulous that tightened her chest.

"You'll like Karen," he said. "She's calm and low-key. I've already approved the questions."

"You *approved* my questions?" Joan tried to sharpen her tone, but it was hard to stay angry with somebody who was so thorough. She might not agree with his methods, but there was no doubting his loyalty and sincerity.

He nodded. "Five minutes, Joan. Let them see you. Let them hear you. And I promise you won't be forbidden fruit anymore."

"My parents—"

The sale clerk reappeared. "Can I get your signature, Mr. Verdun?"

He signed the slip. "Your parents will be proud."

"My parents will be angry."

The sales clerk walked away.

"They want this to die down, right?"

"Of course they want it to die down," said Joan. They wanted it to die down in the most expedient fashion possible.

"Then do the interview. Don't be forbidden fruit anymore."

Joan understood his logic. She didn't want to agree with it, but she understood it. "What about Heather?"

"Heather will be tied up in mud wraps and massages until at least five."

"How do you know that?"

"Because I don't leave things to chance."

Joan's eyes narrowed. Was he saying…? "You bribed the salon?"

He nodded. "Absolutely."

Joan glanced around the store. "So you just played me?"

"Get your other clothes."

"No."

"We're going to be late."

"I haven't even said yes."

He put a hand on the small of her back and urged her toward the changing room. "But you will." He paused. "You're a smart woman, Joan. I don't represent dummies."

"And you're a devious man, Anthony." She liked the feel of his hand on her back. She resisted just enough so he'd keep it there.

"That's what you pay me for."

"I don't pay you to be devious."

"You pay me to look after your best interests."

She stopped and turned to look into his eyes, a buzzing sexual arousal combining with a truth she'd never faced before. "I didn't realize I was paying you to do my dirty work."

"We set up an offshore account through three numbered holding companies. What did you think I was doing?"

Her voice went husky in a moment of pure honesty. "Protecting me."

His palm slipped ever so slightly down the curve of her spine. "I'm still protecting you, Joan. This interview is the best way I know to protect you."

She remembered his solid presence in her living room last night when he'd planted himself between her and potential danger. *They go through me to get to you,* he'd said. Right now, watching his eyes darken to a midnight sky, she believed every word.

ANTHONY WORKED to quell his nerves as he watched Joan through the control room window. Clearly thrilled with the opportunity, Karen St. Claire peppered her with friendly, chatty questions about her story ideas and her quiet lifestyle in Indigo.

They'd met with Ray and Karen before the interview, making sure everyone was clear on the rules. Still, Anthony could tell Joan was nervous by the way she twisted her little ruby ring around and around her finger, but she was doing a fabulous job. She smiled openly at Karen, answered the questions directly and articulately, leaving just enough to the imagination. If he'd known she was this poised and beautiful in front of the cameras, he'd have pushed her on publicity a lot harder a lot sooner.

The five-minute mark went by, but nobody made any

move to shut it down. If the networks were still carrying the interview, this was the publicity coup of a lifetime. He could see daytime talk shows in their future.

"Were you angry when the Prism Agency leaked your name?" Karen asked.

Anthony tensed. It was the first question that wasn't on his approved list.

Joan's smile didn't falter. "Not at all, Karen. Anthony Verdun and I keep in very close touch, and the move didn't surprise me."

Brilliant. And it was the third time she'd dropped Anthony's name. He owed her big-time.

"Are you saying you authorized the release of your identity?"

"Mr. Verdun works within parameters that allow him to make the best choices for my career on a wide range of issues."

Anthony could barely sit still. She was good. She was better than good. His cell phone vibrated against his chest, but he ignored it.

He vaguely heard the booth door open behind him. He ignored that, too.

Then Heather's voice hissed in his ear. "You *set me up*."

He spared her a sideways glance. "I merely distracted you."

"You're an evil little man."

Anthony glanced through the window to the hallway. He and Joan had gone through two separate security checks. "How'd you get in here?"

Heather crossed her arms and gave him an imperious look. "You're joking, right?"

He took in her clothes, her hair, her makeup and a

demeanor that had wealth and breeding stamped all over it. Silly question. Heather could get into the inner sanctum of the CIA if she put her mind to it.

"She's doing great," he said, nodding to Joan.

"What great?" Incredulity crept into Heather's hushed voice. "I call Samuel Kane off the tabloids yesterday, only to have you stuff her in front of a camera today?"

"This is different."

"No. It's not."

Not that he owed Heather any explanation. "I picked the interviewer. I approved the questions."

"You're throwing her to the wolves to further your own interests."

"Karen St. Claire is hardly the wolves." Anthony's phone vibrated again.

"You hurt my sister, and I'll hunt you down."

The threat didn't worry him. Not that Heather couldn't have him killed, or worse. He simply had no intention of hurting Joan.

Out in the studio, Karen St. Claire straightened the index cards on the news desk in front of her. "Can you tell us a little about your late husband?"

Joan's expression faltered, and Anthony jumped up. "End it," he called to the news director.

The news director signaled to Karen, and she smoothly wrapped it up.

The second they switched to a commercial, Anthony was through the booth door. He brushed his way past cameras and assistants, stepping over extension cords to get to Joan just as she removed her microphone.

He drew her into his arms and hugged her tight

to his chest. "You were magnificent," he mumbled in her ear.

She molded against him, and he prolonged the hug, greedily absorbing her essence.

"Did he drug you or something?" asked Heather.

"Thirty seconds," said the producer. "Can we clear the set, please?"

One arm still around Joan, Anthony made his way through the set drapes to the studio door.

"Seriously," said Heather, as she scrambled along behind them. "Joanie, how did he talk you into it?"

"He was right," said Joan, and Anthony tightened his arm on her. "Playing hard to get only makes them more interested."

"That's men, not the general public," said Heather as the door closed behind them and they started down the dark, narrow hallway that led to the green room.

"Principle's the same," said Anthony.

"He's only trying to make money," Heather accused.

"While you're trying to stuff the genie back in the bottle," said Anthony.

"I'm your sister, and I love you," said Heather.

"Then call up your parents." Anthony whisked Joan through the lobby, under the interested gazes of the studio staff. "Call up your friends. Tell them that Joan is an excellent writer, and they should all buy her books."

"It's not that simple," Heather objected.

"It's not that simple," Joan agreed as they exited through the double glass doors.

Anthony knew he'd gone one step too far. Joan was aligning herself with Heather again, when he needed her to trust him.

He cursed himself silently. There was no doubt in his mind they'd get more interview offers. He needed her to be ready, and he needed her to be willing.

JOAN WAS STILL feeling buoyed when Anthony pulled into her short driveway in Indigo. The interview was over. Soon the hype would die down, Anthony would go back to New York, and she could get back to normal again.

She still felt uneasy at the thought of talking to her parents. But at least she could tell them they were past the publicity peak. Things would only calm down from here.

Her stomach fluttered at the thought of Anthony leaving, but she ignored that. He was her agent, not her best friend. They'd go back to talking on the phone every month or so. She could even fantasize about him in the dead of night—just as she'd done for years, ever since Brian had turned into a warm but distant memory.

Normalcy. How she craved it right now.

"Thank God we're home," moaned Heather from the cramped backseat. "My massage has been completely obliterated." She stretched her neck back and forth.

Anthony shut down the engine, set the brake and opened his door. He unfolded his body and flipped the seat forward so Heather could escape.

Joan hopped out her own side and retrieved her purse and the boutique bag from the floor behind her.

"You left your door open," said Heather.

Joan pushed it shut. "Give me a second here."

"No. I mean that one." Heather pointed to the house. "Your front door is open."

Anthony stilled, twisting his head toward the house. "Stay here," he ordered.

"It was probably just the wind," said Joan, but an unsettling twinge shot up her spine. In ten years of storms off the Gulf, her door had never once blown open.

"I'm not staying out here," said Heather, trotting behind Anthony.

Joan rounded the hood of the car, following suit. She wasn't timid like Heather, but it was dark now and she didn't relish the thought of standing outside amid the sound of the cicadas and sway of the hanging moss, wondering what might be lurking around the cypress trees.

Anthony strode up the stairs to the open doorway.

"You should really get a gun," Heather muttered.

"Quiet," said Anthony. He paused in the doorway and cocked his head.

Joan could hear the ticking clock, the gentle hum of the fridge motor and the wind rustling the oak leaves— no footfalls, no voices.

Anthony stepped inside. The floor creaked under his shoes. He reached to the right and flipped a light switch.

Joan blinked at the bright light, then gasped as the room came into focus.

Her bookcase had been tipped over, and papers were strewn across the living room floor. The kitchen looked intact, but her writing nook was in complete disarray. Worst of all, there was a gaping hole where her computer had stood.

Anthony reached for his phone and dialed 911.

"I need to look upstairs," said Joan, moving around Anthony. She kept backup disks in her bedroom closet.

Anthony grabbed her by the arm and pinned her to his side. "This is Anthony Verdun," he said into the phone. "I'm at Joan Bateman's house on Amelie Lane. There's been a robbery." He paused. "Yes." Another pause. "I think they're gone. Okay. We will."

He closed the phone.

"You are not going anywhere," he said to Joan.

"My backup disks," she told him. "They're in my bedroom." She had to know if her work was safe. That computer represented hours and days and months of her life. She had a manuscript in progress and hundreds of research files stored on it.

If anybody could understand her panic, it was Anthony.

He glanced at her writing nook and gritted his teeth. "Okay."

"Okay?" Heather shrieked. "You're going to risk her neck for the backup disks?"

"I'll go first," said Anthony.

"Wait for the police," said Heather. *"They* have guns."

Anthony glared disdainfully down at her. "I can take care of myself."

"I don't care about you. I care about Joan."

"I'm not going to let anything happen to Joan."

Heather folded her arms over her chest. "Of course you won't. She's your meal ticket."

Joan was mortified. *"Heather!"*

"Do the interview," Heather mimicked. "Do the interview and everything will be all right. Does this look all right to you?"

Joan went cold. The interview. Could the break-in have something to do with the interview?

She scanned the disordered room once more. Priceless works of art were left untouched. Her hall closet door was closed. The kitchen hadn't been disturbed. Only her desk. Her computer. Her writing.

She blinked up at Anthony. "Is this because of the interview?"

"No," he said. But she could tell he wasn't completely sure.

Joan backed away from him.

He'd been wrong.

She'd been wrong.

She should have gone with her own instincts and stayed out of the limelight. This would probably make the news, too. Soon her father would be storming Indigo with court orders and bodyguards.

She felt Heather's thin arm go around her. "We'll go to Paris," her sister whispered.

Joan's heart-rate sped up, and her breathing deepened. Maybe she should have gone to Paris in the first place.

POLICE CHIEF Alain Boudreaux concluded what Anthony had already guessed. A fan had broken in looking for souvenirs. One of the neighbors had reported a cluster of people in front of Joan's house while they were away in Lafayette. And there were several gushing messages on Joan's answering machine.

A fan was a whole lot better than a psychopathic criminal, and it was unlikely the fan would be back now that he had the souvenirs. Still, Anthony wasn't taking any chances with Joan and Heather's safety.

Over their halfhearted protests, he checked them both into La Petite Maison, Heather on the second floor and Joan in the attic suite.

"You don't need to stay," said Joan, sitting primly

in the rocking chair in the corner of her room. The French doors were open to the small balcony, and the oak leaves rustled in the midnight breeze.

"I don't want to go," said Anthony honestly. It had been a long, roller-coaster of a day for both of them.

Their host, Luc Carter, had settled Heather into her room and promised to double lock the front door. Anthony's room was directly below Joan's, next to the attic staircase, and he fully intended to keep his door open all night long. Still, he wasn't ready to have her out of his sight just yet.

"Alain said the break-in happened this morning." Anthony was desperate to get the cool, distant look out of Joan's eyes.

She darted him a glare. "You're staying to *defend* yourself?"

He moved to the wicker chair that was positioned on the opposite side of the stone fireplace. "I'm staying because I'm worried about you. I'm simply pointing out—for future reference—that the interview and the break-in were two separate events."

She started rocking. "Right. Who knows what kind of sicko a national television spot will bring out of the woodwork."

"Joan."

"Do you know what Alain just asked me?"

"What?"

"He asked me to endorse the music festival."

The change of topic was abrupt, but Anthony didn't point that out. His mind started clicking through the promotional opportunities of the music festival. He should give Lesley Roland a call. She was one of the best publicists in the business.

"Stop!"

He glanced up. "What?"

"You're already scheming." Joan stood up and took a couple of paces forward. "I'm *not* endorsing the music festival. I don't *want* the music festival."

He stood with her. "Why not?"

"It'll ruin the town. Crowds will converge—"

"It's Cajun culture at the old opera house. We're not talking heavy metal."

She folded her arms over her chest. "And it would be good for my career."

Anthony moved in front of her. "What's wrong with something being good for your career? Publicity is not a four-letter word."

Her cheeks flushed, and her green eyes smoldered in the dim light. "Just once I'd like you to think about what would be good for my *life* instead of my career."

"They're not mutually exclusive."

She waved a hand. "It's all about the sales to you."

"That's because I'm your agent."

"Yeah? Well…" She bit her bottom lip, and her eyes clouded as the sound of the cicadas rose. The temperature in the room spiked, even while the breeze wafted moisture-laced air from the bayou.

He thought she swayed toward him.

Was she feeling half of what he was feeling?

He stared into the depths of her eyes.

"You want me to be something else, Joan?" he dared.

She blinked her lashes but didn't say a word.

A weight pressed down on his chest.

Slowly, knowing it was crazy, knowing he was losing his mind, he raised his hand to touch her soft cheek.

Even as his brain screamed at him to stop, his fingers tunneled into her thick hair.

Her lips parted as she sucked in a breath, and her eyes fluttered closed, dark lashes sensual against the dewy glow of her skin.

He cupped her face with his other hand, drawing her toward him in slow motion. Ten years of pent-up desire simmered to life within him, threatening to overwhelm him, dragging him into oblivion. A taste, he promised himself. Nothing more than a taste of her tender lips.

She tipped her head.

It was all the invitation he needed.

His lips came down on hers, and paradise ricocheted through every cell in his body. His hands convulsed into her hair. His lips parted, his tongue flicking ever so lightly against her mouth. He moaned with the supreme effort it took to hold back.

She stepped forward, and her thighs brushed against him. He drew her in tight, his mouth widening, turning an exploratory kiss into one of absolute carnality. His palm slipped down to the small of her back, and he pressed her against his erection.

Her arms wound around his neck as she accepted his kisses, opening wider, allowing him to taste the secret caverns of her mouth. Her tongue answered his plea, and he felt the sultry night settle around them.

The feather bed was mere feet away.

He wanted her naked on the cool, crisp comforter.

He wanted her shimmering hair splayed out against the white pillowcase.

He wanted to hold her, and kiss her, and make her his own.

It was Joan in his arms. It was Joan whom he'd

dreamed about forever. The scent and feel and taste of her overwhelmed his senses. He kissed her cheek, her neck, the tender skin over her collarbone. He ran his hands up her sides, skimming the mound of her breasts, longing to strip away the prim jacket and blouse and find his way to the real woman.

"Anthony," she breathed.

He slipped the jeweled jacket from her shoulders. "Yeah?"

Her arms tightened on his neck, and her lips returned to his. Her breasts pressed against his chest, soft and malleable, the stuff of his fantasies.

She moaned softly. "This is…"

"I know." They had to stop. But he couldn't for the life of him figure out how. He promised himself just one more minute of heaven. Then he'd pull back. Then he'd become her agent once more.

He drew her bottom lip into his mouth. She tasted of dark secrets and smooth, southern nectar.

He wanted her. He needed her. He let his fingertip brush the small strip of skin between her skirt and her silk blouse. He was instantly pitched to a new height of arousal.

Panic invaded his system. He wasn't going to be able to let her go. He'd keep going and going until there was nothing left between them. Nothing but—

With a burst of iron will, he drew back.

She blinked, obviously disoriented.

"I'm sorry," he whispered, telling himself to step away before he started all over again.

"Sorry?" she parroted.

He backed off a little more. "That shouldn't have happened."

"Because you're my agent?"

He dropped his hands to his sides and retreated a good two feet. "Because that's not how it's supposed to be between us."

She nodded shakily. "You're supposed to sell my books and fight with me about publicity."

He nodded. "That's right." His judgment was already clouded enough when it came to Joan.

The interview this afternoon had been the right thing to do on so many levels. But he found himself second-guessing that decision. He found himself second-guessing so much when it came to her. He needed to focus. He couldn't do the right thing for her if his emotions got mixed up with his logic.

Despite her protests, she needed an agent. She needed an agent now more than ever. And it was his responsibility to take care of business.

"I'll be right downstairs," he told her.

She nodded again.

"You're perfectly safe."

"I know."

"But my door is open."

"Okay."

"If you need anything."

She was so incredibly gorgeous and so incredibly vulnerable standing there in the hot night.

His fingers shook with the effort it took to keep away from her. He had to get out fast. He curled his hands into fists as he turned away.

Her soft voice puffed on the breeze. "Stay."

Oh, God.

CHAPTER SIX

HEATHER WASN'T NORMALLY an early riser. But then this wasn't a normal day. And she supposed, technically, this wasn't rising early anyway. It was staying up very, very late.

She'd tossed and turned all night, alternately worrying about the family's reputation and Joan's physical safety. If fans were willing to break into her house for her computer, what else were they willing to do? Was her sister going to end up like Elvis, a recluse hiding out from the world for the rest of her life?

And what would this mean for their parents? Heather hadn't been brave enough to call them yet. She definitely didn't have any good news to report.

Her sister had written more than a dozen mystery books. She showed no signs of heading for Europe. And she had fallen under the power of an evil publicity hound of an agent.

That wasn't even touching the bondage scene. Heather shuddered at the very thought.

By 6 a.m., Heather had to get out of the B and B. She needed some air. She needed to clear her head.

She started walking and found herself on Joan's street. She stopped in front of Joan's cottage, staring at that ominous, wide-open front door.

She'd kidnap Joan if need be, she vowed. But they were heading back to Boston today, and they were hiring the best security firm money could buy. Anthony might not be bragging when he said he could take care of himself, but Heather wasn't trusting him with Joan's life.

Suddenly, there was a loud bang from inside the cottage.

Heather froze, a chill of fear working its way up her spine. She remembered Alain Boudreaux had secured the front door last night. Would the police have come back this early?

She glanced up and down the street. But there were no cruisers to be seen, no help of any kind, for that matter. The lane was empty as far as she could see.

She took a shaky step backward. Whoever was in there, she wasn't about to confront them alone. But then a dark figure appeared in the doorway, and she lost the feeling in her legs.

"Heather?"

It was Samuel.

Samuel.

Her breath rushed out of her along with her strength. She was safe.

He started down the stairs.

Wait a minute.

What was Samuel doing here? Could he have been the one who broke into the cottage yesterday? He had cause to be angry with Joan. Did that give him a reason to take her computer? Had his plan all along been to go to the press?

"Heather?" he repeated when she didn't answer. He reached the bottom of the stairs and started down the walkway.

She swallowed her suspicions, not afraid of him. Not really. "Hello, Samuel."

He closed the distance between them. "What are you doing here?" He stopped in front of her, a six-foot-four wall of muscle.

"I'm out walking."

His eyes narrowed. "Why?"

"I couldn't sleep."

He stared at her in silence, while she tried to decipher his expression. Was he angry? Nervous? Did he mean her harm?

Finally, she couldn't stand it anymore. "And what are *you* doing…here?"

"Returning to the scene of the crime."

She took a step back. "Oh."

His mouth crooked into a half smile, his teeth white and straight against his dark complexion. "Relax, Heather. It wasn't my crime."

"Never thought it was.

"You are such an easy mark."

"I am not."

"You presumed I was guilty. Again."

She shook her head in denial, even though it was true. There was something about Samuel that made it easy to believe he could be on the wrong side of the law.

"Alain called me because somebody broke into my house, too."

That surprised her. "Really?"

"Yes, really. Disappointed that I'm not a thief?"

"Of course not."

"You look a little disappointed."

"Don't be ridiculous."

He waggled his eyebrows. "You've got a bad-boy fetish."

She glared up at him. "You wish."

"No, I know."

"I don't have a fetish of any kind."

"Everybody's got a fetish."

She shook her head emphatically. "Not me."

"Let me guess," he drawled. "The missionary position."

She squared her shoulders. "That is none of your business." She couldn't believe he'd even asked.

"In the dark."

"I am not answering that question."

"I'll take that as a yes."

"I don't care what you take it as." Quite frankly, there was nothing wrong with the missionary position. And there was nothing wrong with having sex in the dark. The dark was soft and romantic, it camouflaged flaws and allowed a person to focus on sensation.

"You really need to get out more," he drawled.

"I live in Boston." How dare a backwoods Indigo carpenter insinuate she wasn't worldly.

He shrugged. "Too bad they don't have good sex in Boston."

Heather flattened her lips and warmed up for a scathing diatribe. But then she saw the laughter lurking behind his eyes. Oh no, he wasn't going to win this one.

"Why don't we talk about *your* sex life for a while?" she suggested smoothly.

"I don't talk about my sex life." His dark eyes glowed with raw sensuality, while his voice dropped to a throbbing bass. "But I'd be happy to give you a free demonstration."

A hot rush flared from the pit of her stomach. "I can't believe you said that."

"And I can't believe you blushed."

"That's shock and disbelief."

"You sure?"

No, she wasn't sure. Her traitorous body was showing all the signs of arousal. Stupid body. Definitely time to get the heck out of this conversation. "Why don't you tell me what they took?"

"Who?"

"Whoever broke into your house."

"Nothing."

"What do you mean, nothing? Nobody breaks into a house and takes nothing."

"You accusing me of lying?"

Yes. "No."

There wasn't a doubt in Heather's mind that Samuel would lie. Probably recreationally, certainly if it would gain him something.

The sound of tires and a car engine put off his response. Heather turned to see a black, panel-sided van round the corner. The satellite dish on the roof could mean only one thing, and she groaned out loud.

It rocked to a halt beside them, the door immediately sliding open, while a thirtyish man with slicked hair and an angular face hopped out. He wore khaki slacks and short-sleeved dress shirt. And he carried a microphone.

"Joan Bateman?" he asked, stuffing it in her face.

Heather shook her head, but she knew better than to utter a single word.

Samuel smoothly but firmly positioned his body between them. Then he urged her back with his broad palm. Her stomach contracted under his touch, but she moved the way he guided.

"I'm looking for Joan Bateman," said the reporter, glancing around in eager expectation.

"She's not here," said Samuel.

"And you are?"

Samuel didn't answer.

"He's Samuel Kane," shrieked a woman from the driver's seat, clattering into the back of the van on high heels. "That old murder-suicide. He's her muse."

"You're Samuel Kane?" asked the reporter.

"What about it?"

The man's focus snagged on Samuel, and he thrust the microphone forward again. "Do you agree with Joan Bateman's version of your parents' murders?"

"I don't know," said Samuel in an impressively neutral tone. "I haven't read the book."

Oh yeah. Samuel could lie, all right. He could take the witness stand for her any old time.

"But you think your father was innocent?"

"So I've said. Many times." Samuel turned and linked Heather's arm, pulling her along as he walked away.

"Do you think your father was framed?" the reporter called after them.

Samuel headed for the driveway, and Heather struggled to keep up. She could feel the tension in the muscles of his forearms.

"Where are we going?" she demanded under her breath.

"Mr. Kane?" The reporter caught up with them. "Do you have any comment on the theory that your father was framed?"

Samuel stopped. His jaw hardened. He turned and pasted the man with a menacing glare, holding his ground, leaning slightly forward.

The reporter opened his mouth.

Samuel raised his eyebrow.

"Thank you," the reporter sputtered as he backed off.

"Wow," said Heather.

"There should be a law against that."

She'd been talking about Samuel's ability to make grown men run for cover, but she didn't correct him.

"My truck's around the side," he said. "You want a lift?"

Heather nodded. "Yes. Please."

She needed to warn Joan about the reporters. And she needed to warn her about Samuel's comments. And she'd better get on the phone to her parents, quick. Joan's interview was one thing, but if they caught her and Samuel on the evening news, there was going to be a whole lot more explaining to do.

THE ONLY GOOD THING about Heather's story was that it acted as a buffer between Joan and Anthony over breakfast. Bad enough that she'd kissed him last night. Okay, so *kiss* was probably too mild a word. She'd practically made love to him with her mouth.

But then she'd called him back.

He was almost to the door, and she'd practically begged him to stay. Luckily, he was smart enough for both of them and kept going. Which made the morning after even worse.

"You have to call Mom," said Heather, taking another drink of her coffee but ignoring the fresh croissant on the plate in front of her.

Joan shook her head. "I'm not calling Mom."

"It's your book."

"You're the spy. You report in to headquarters."

Anthony interrupted with a harsh sigh. "You are both grown women. Will you start acting like it?"

Joan looked at him for the first time. "Excuse me?"

He set down his coffee cup. "Call your parents, already."

"Like you would."

"Of course I would."

"With disastrous news."

"In my family, this wouldn't *be* disastrous news."

"Oh, and they'd be *so* happy to have you publicly involved in a sordid murder inquest?"

Anthony took his napkin from his lap and tossed it on the table. "They'd be happy to see me succeeding at something as tough and competitive as fiction writing."

Joan knew he was trying to manipulate her. "And their friends, their colleagues, their social contacts—"

"Would be happy for me, too."

"Yeah, right."

"Honestly, Joan. I don't know what kind of world you two grew up in."

Low blow. She glared at him.

"But you people have some serious issues."

Luc Carter strode in through the doorway. "You guys better take a look at this," he said, turning on a small television on the countertop.

Anthony came to his feet as Samuel and Heather appeared on the screen. "Turn it up."

Heather groaned. "Look at my hair!"

"It's fine," Joan lied, glancing sideways at her sister.

Heather on television with bed head. What were the odds?

"Shhh," said Anthony.

"I already told you what we said," Heather put in.

The shot of Samuel's angry scowl faded from the screen, and the announcer reappeared, smoothly segueing into the next story.

"You'll probably want to call Mom now," said Heather.

Joan closed her eyes and struggled to come up with a spin, *any* spin that would make the situation sound better.

Thing is, Mom, I'm a closet mystery writer. There's a bondage scene in my latest novel. And the funniest part, it's based on this murder-suicide...

Okay. That sure wasn't it.

Anthony's cell phone rang, but instead of answering it, he focused on Joan across the table. "You okay?"

"I'm perfect."

His phone rang again, but he continued to hold her gaze.

He was obviously worried about her. She'd seen that look a hundred times. But something had changed. After last night, there was a wall of hesitation between them.

He didn't seem to know how he should act.

Well, she sure didn't know how she should act, either.

The phone rang a third time.

"Excuse me," he finally said with obvious reluctance. He turned and walked through the doorway to the public lounge, flipping open his phone. "Verdun here."

"Wow," said Heather, as Luc shut off the television

and followed Anthony out of the breakfast room. "Forget calling Mom."

Joan felt a small ray of hope. "You'll do it?"

Heather shook her head. "No. I want to talk about Anthony."

"What about Anthony?"

"What's going on between the two of you? I've got a nose for tension, and *wow.*"

"There's no tension between us," Joan lied, even as the tension buzzed its way through her limbs. Last night might have been a bigger mistake than she realized. Where did their relationship go now?

Heather shook her head, moved forward and lowered her voice. "What on earth did I miss?"

"Nothing," said Joan, staring her sister straight in the eye.

"You lie."

"I'm calling Mom."

"Okay, now I *know* it's something big. Did you sleep with him? Huh?"

"No, I didn't sleep with him." Joan headed for the phone in the corner of the breakfast room, but Heather followed on her heels.

"Because yesterday you two were all chummy and touchy."

"We weren't touchy."

"Oh, yes, you were."

"Well, a few things have changed since yesterday." The interview, for one. The break-in, for another. The kiss…Joan silently groaned.

"And now you both act like you're going to jump out of your skin."

Joan lifted the receiver and pressed the Talk button.

"You're imagining things." She punched in her long distance access number.

Heather shook her head and clicked her tongue. "I'm not imagining things. I'm observant and perceptive, remember?"

Joan keyed in her calling card. "You mean delusional."

"What did he do?"

"Nothing."

"Then what did you do?"

"Nothing, either."

"You were still together when Luc and I left your room."

"So what?" At the prompt, Joan dialed her parents' number.

"Alone…in that romantic attic suite…"

"And Anthony left about five minutes later."

"A lot can happen in five minutes."

A ring tone sounded in Joan's ear. "Or very little can happen in five minutes."

"Joanie?"

"Yeah?"

"While we've been talking…"

Joan waited.

"You dialed Mom."

Joan swore under her breath The receiver suddenly felt like a lead weight in her hands.

"Bateman residence," came Dinora's voice.

"GET HER BACK out in front of the cameras right now," boomed Stephen Baker.

"She's not ready," Anthony returned, glancing up to make sure Joan and Heather were still occupied in the breakfast room.

"I'm standing now," said Stephen. "My blood pressure just went up thirty points."

"The news story alone will sell thousands of copies," Anthony pointed out. Stephen might think the sky was the limit on publicity, but Anthony had Joan's feelings to worry about.

She'd been through a lot in the past two days. And he wasn't forcing her into anything. Not that he could force her, in any case. Not that he had any right to even ask, since he'd shattered a pretty rigid professional boundary last night.

He shuddered to think what might have happened if he'd listened to the soft plea in her voice—if he'd gone back. He knew that if he'd so much as turned around and looked at her, he'd have plunged headlong into that big bed and lost himself in her luscious body. And then things would have been even more awkward this morning.

"I'm taking a nitro pill," growled Stephen.

"I have a plan," said Anthony. He had to think. There had to be a way to appease Stephen while respecting Joan's desire for privacy.

Stephen's voice rose. "*What* plan? I don't see our star author on a morning talk show. Do you? You need to return Charlie Long's phone call right away."

"We need to let things calm down first."

"What calm down? We want to heat them up." If the tone of Stephen's voice was anything to go by, the man might truly be on the verge of a heart attack.

"She's been through a lot," said Anthony.

"She's not made of spun glass," Stephen returned.

Anthony paused, gritting his teeth. "Give me some time."

"I'll come to Indigo—"

"*No!*"

A new voice came on the line. "Anthony?"

"Yes?"

"Bo Reese here."

Anthony froze. Pellegrin Publishing's vice-president was in Stephen's office?

"Anthony?"

"Hello, Mr. Reese."

The man laughed. "Bo, please."

"Bo," said Anthony, struggling to get his bearings.

"How are things going down there?" Bo asked heartily.

"It's one of my more interesting trips," Anthony admitted, glancing into the breakfast room again. Still no sign of Joan or Heather.

"Could have knocked us over with a feather when we found out Jules Burrell was a woman."

"Quite a few people were surprised," said Anthony, bracing for Bo to start the hard sell.

"We're looking at bringing out her backlist."

"Sounds great," said Anthony, relaxing ever so slightly. Joan's backlist was an untapped gold mine for all of them.

"Can somebody fax me copies of her original contracts?" he asked. He was making sure the publisher stuck to every single provision he'd negotiated for reprints.

Bo chuckled again. "Of course we can."

"I'll read them over before we talk further."

"Always an eye on business," said Bo.

"I like to think so."

"Here's the thing."

Anthony braced himself.

"*Bayou Betrayal* is shaping up for a placement of at least twenty-five or thirty on the *New York Times* list."

Anthony struggled to quell a surge of excitement. He had a best-selling author. Professionally, this was phenomenal.

"With the right circumstances," Bo continued, "she might break the top ten."

Now Anthony struggled not to hyperventilate.

"And then there's the backlist. We're prepared to launch a national media campaign, volume discounts, premium store placement, and any book tour she cares to name."

This was it. This was the big time. For him, for Joan, for Prism.

"What do you say we start the ball rolling with Charlie Long?"

Anthony's stomach congealed. They had him.

Of course they'd want the talk shows. They needed the talk shows. And Joan needed the talk shows, too.

Opportunities like this were lightning strikes, fleeting and never to be repeated. A couple of days from now, the news cycle would move on, and Joan would be out in the cold.

"I'll do my best," he heard himself say, struggling to come up with a strategy he could sell to her.

"*Fantastic,*" said Bo. "You know, Anthony, if it would help…we could see if Charlie's willing to make the call personally."

Anthony hesitated. Ask Charlie Long to contact Joan? It was a risk. But it might be the only thing that would sway her.

He drew a deep breath.

"We've done it before," said Bo.

"Fine," said Anthony, gritting his teeth. "No harm in asking if he's willing."

CHAPTER SEVEN

JOAN FELT as if she were fourteen years old all over again. It happened every time she upset her mother. Normally, she tried very hard not to upset her mother.

"Because it's the only way to nip this untenable situation in the bud," her mother said tartly.

"If we give them some time," Joan tried, "people might get used to the idea."

She'd already apologized in half a dozen ways, but there was no backpedalling from this one. Going forward was her only hope.

Her mother's voice rose. "We don't want them to *get used* to the idea. We want them to forget all about the idea. You had to know this couldn't end well."

"I didn't think much about the ending," Joan confessed, tracing her finger along the outline of the wildflower pattern on the breakfast room wallpaper.

If only *The New York Times* hadn't picked up the story. If only Samuel hadn't gone in front of the cameras. And if only she hadn't included that bondage scene in *Bayou Betrayal*. She then might have had a chance to smooth things over.

But all those ships had sailed.

Paris was looking better and better. Maybe she could find a little garret off the Champs Élysées and come up with a different pen name. She sighed at the thought of starting everything from scratch. But what was her choice?

"This is all so typically you," her mother sighed. "Plunging into some wild scheme without giving a single thought to the consequences. It's like the time you played piano for that awful rock and roll band, and we had to—"

"I'll go to Paris, Mom." Joan glanced up just in time to see Anthony freeze in the breakfast room doorway, cell phone in his hand.

There was a pregnant pause all around.

Her mother was the first to break it. "Now you're making some sense," she enthused.

Anthony shook his head, and his voice went hoarse. "No." He took a jerky step forward, but Heather moved in front of him.

"I'll get your father to call the pilot right away," said her mother.

Joan shrank against the sideboard as Anthony tried to jockey his way around Heather without manhandling her.

"I have to go, Mom," said Joan.

"But we need to make plans," her mother complained.

"Get out of my way," Anthony growled.

"She's going to Paris," said Heather.

"Heather said the jet could land at St. Martinville." Her mother's words sped up. "I'd suggest you—"

"We can go commercial," said Joan.

"Don't be ridiculous."

Anthony grasped Heather by the shoulders and all but lifted her out of the way.

"Gotta go, Mom."

"But—"

Joan disconnected.

Anthony stopped in front of her, his breathing deep, neck muscles pumped. "We have to talk.".

"She's going to Paris," Heather repeated.

"Outside," said Anthony.

"Don't do it, Joanie."

Joan leaned around Anthony to look at her sister. "We're just going to talk."

"I don't trust him."

Joan rolled her eyes. She owed Anthony an explanation. She'd tell him reasonably and rationally that she wasn't willing to hurt her family. She'd never sought fame in the past, and she didn't want it now.

Sure, the interview yesterday had been a bit of a lark. There were even parts of it that she'd enjoyed. And, although she'd never admit it to another living soul, the crew and the interviewer's enthusiasm at meeting her were a nice little ego boost.

She'd lived in her father's shadow, her mother's shadow, even Heather's shadow her whole life. For once it had just been her. "Joan," they'd called her, not Conrad Bateman's daughter or Heather's sister. Just Joan.

She almost sighed in regret, but quickly brought herself back to reality. She'd caused this problem. She had to fix it.

"We can talk outside," she said to Anthony.

"What about the reporters?" asked Heather. "The fans? There are people out in the lane."

"I ordered them off the property," Luc put in.

"We'll go down to the gazebo," said Joan, wanting to get it over with. "It's private."

Anthony latched on to her arm. "Let's go."

"They'll see you."

Luc's voice overrode Heather's. "Only access is through the B and B. They'll be safe."

"This is *none* of your business," said Heather.

"Fair enough," said Luc. "But they can still use the gazebo."

Heather's expression of outrage almost made Joan smile. But she couldn't smile. Not right now. Disappointing Anthony chilled her in some deep corner of her soul.

"Let's go," he said, and she moved into step beside him.

A set of French doors led to the porch, where a white, wooden staircase took them down to the stone path that wound its way to the old gazebo.

They walked in silence, but Joan could feel the tension radiating from Anthony's body. After about two minutes, they entered a grove of oaks. The sunlight turned dappled, and the sounds of the birds and frogs on the bayou rose around them.

The gazebo came into view, and Anthony stopped abruptly. He turned. "Is this about the kiss?"

The question took Joan by surprise. She'd been trying to forget the stupid kiss. "No. But how kind of you to bring it up."

He raked a hand through his hair, and his blue eyes bored intently into hers. "Because I'm sorry about that, okay?"

"You're sorry you kissed me?" Wasn't that just what every woman wanted to hear?

He clenched his fists. "Of course I'm sorry."

She tried not to let his words wound her. "I see.

Thank you for clarifying that. I'd hate to have left the country thinking—"

"Joan."

"What?" she snapped. So much for being reasonable and rational. As usual, it took all of thirty seconds for Anthony to make her crazy.

His voice turned husky. "It was a mistake. A very big mistake."

"I got it, Anthony." She really got it. She'd made a fool of herself last night. "I'll go to Paris."

"Now *that* would be an even bigger mistake," he said.

"Yeah? Well, I guess it's my turn to make one, isn't it?"

"Your mother is trying to torpedo your career."

"Leave my mother out of this."

"How can I leave her out of it? She *is* it. You're talking crazy because of your family."

"Don't you—"

"The world is yours, Joan. You can write your own ticket."

"I don't want to write my own ticket. I want to write novels."

"Then write them."

"I will."

"Good."

"In Paris. Under a new pen name."

There was a moment of stunned silence in which the frogs, cicadas and bird calls pressed in around them. Then Anthony's face contorted, and he sputtered something that might have been a word in another language, but it certainly wasn't in English. His complexion darkened, and for a second she thought he might be having a heart attack.

"Anthony?"

He finally breathed. "Do you have *any* idea what you're throwing away?"

"I don't care about the money, Anthony."

"Normal authors *kill* for opportunities like this. They don't throw them out like garbage."

"If people like my writing as Jules Burrell, they'll like it just as well as John Smith."

"That's not the way it works."

"That's the way it's worked so far."

He closed the space between them.

Something splashed in the bayou, and she automatically glanced to see if it was an alligator.

"It's taken you ten years and a dozen books to get any notoriety at all."

She pursed her lips. "I don't want notoriety."

"Notoriety brings sales. Sales bring opportunities, power, options. It's a package deal, Joan. I've—we've—*I've* worked my butt off for ten years."

"Excuse me? Who wrote the books?"

"Without me, they'd still be locked away in your bottom drawer."

That one hurt. It really hurt. "Is that what you honestly think?"

She waited in silence while the afternoon heat flowed restlessly out of the moist ground, and sweat congealed in her pores.

"No," Anthony finally said, and all the fight went out of his voice. "I think you're a genius, Joan. I think you are the finest writer I have ever had the privilege to represent. And right now I want to wring your mother's neck for stealing you away from me."

Joan blinked, at a loss for words. How could she be

his finest writer? Fine writing was Hemingway or Shakespeare. She messed around with edgy little mysteries.

Anthony drew a breath. He moved closer, and his voice dropped. "Why don't they care about you, Joan?"

What an absurd thing to say. "Of course they care about me."

He shook his head. "Everything they've said, everything they've done has been in their interest, not yours."

"That's because I'm the one who made the mistake." Her actions had hurt them. She'd known she was taking a risk in publishing the books; she just hadn't realized how badly it could blow up in her face.

"And what mistake was that?" he asked.

He knew the mistake as well as she did. He was just trying to bait her into another argument.

"They care about me," she repeated.

"They have a funny way of showing it."

"They're trying to protect me."

"From what?"

Joan sighed.

"Seriously, Joan. From success and money?"

"From exploitation."

That shut him up.

"So, that's what you think of me?" he asked.

"No, that's what *they* think of you."

"That I'm exploiting you?"

"I don't think that."

"You just said it."

"Anthony."

He clasped a hand over the back of his neck. "Did you know *Charlie Long Live* has expressed interest in you?"

"How would I know that?"

"Well, they have."

Despite herself, Joan was flattered. Charlie Long was a reputable journalist. His news show didn't sensationalize issues the way cable talk shows did.

"Why would Charlie Long want me?" she asked.

"Because you wrote a good book. Because people are interested in Samuel's story. They've invited you to headline the show."

Joan would be lying if she didn't admit it was tempting. But she knew that was a selfish emotion at work. An appearance on *Charlie Long* would be good for her, and her alone. It would be devastating for her parents.

"I have to stick with my instincts."

He took her hands in his, the slick pads of his thumbs smoothing over her tender knuckles. His voice went gentle. "And what are your instincts telling you now?"

A bead of sweat formed at her temple and trickled down toward her jawline. She took a bracing breath and forced herself to look him straight in the eyes.

Truth was, her instincts were at war with each other. But she told him part of it. "That when the going gets tough, the family has to stick together."

His jaw went tight, and he closed his eyes for a split second. "And what about you and me sticking together?"

"We're not—"

"They're selfish, Joan."

"They're my family." This was a hard decision, a wrenching decision. Why did he have to make it worse?

"That's not a family."

Her spine stiffened. He'd crossed the line with that one. "Really? What is a family, Anthony?"

"People who support you through thick and thin."

"Like your family?"

"Yes."

She laughed then, but the sound was bitter. "Why don't you tell me what your own sainted family would do under these circumstances?"

"My family wouldn't *be* under these circumstances."

"Of *course* they wouldn't," she snapped. "They're too perfect for this."

"Well, they sure wouldn't be ashamed of me. They'd have thrown my first book launch. They'd have bought copies for their friends, acquaintances and coworkers."

"Why? Is everybody they know trailer trash?" The second the words were out of her mouth, Joan cringed in horror.

Anthony's jaw snapped shut. A chill masked his eyes.

She opened her mouth to apologize, but he held up a hand.

"Don't say another word," he ordered

She tried anyway.

"*Joan.*"

She shut her mouth, waiting for him to yell at her. She certainly deserved it.

But he stood there for a long, silent moment, staring at her as if she were a stranger. Then he turned on his heel to stalk back down the pathway.

Joan didn't move. The splashing in the bayou increased, and she began to hope it was a gator. A big, hungry gator would put an end to all of her problems. Snap, snap, swallow, and she would stop letting everybody down.

IT WAS a long day for Heather. Joan spent most of it in her room, giving only one word answers when Heather called through the door. But since the family jet was booked for their Paris flight tomorrow, and since Joan wasn't talking about canceling their plans, Heather decided to leave well enough alone.

Anthony made himself scarce, and even Luc was busy working on the dock. The number of fans and reporters milling around Indigo was increasing, so Heather didn't really want to venture into town. Out of desperation, she picked up Luc's copy of *Bayou Betrayal.*

She started reading around four o'clock. By six, she was cloistered in her room, riveted by the tension, the plot twists and even the sex in the story. Lost in the characterization, she forgot completely that it had been written by her sister.

Then, sometime in the evening, she heard Samuel's deep voice in the downstairs lounge. It sent a jolt through her stomach and increased her pulse.

She felt the usual sexual buzz in response to him, but her heart also went out to the man. She didn't know how much of *Bayou Betrayal* was true and how much was fiction. But Samuel was definitely Jared, the sixteen-year-old boy who had lost his parents to a horrible crime.

She could see now why Samuel had turned out so tough. He'd stayed in his family cottage all on his own, worked in the evenings during high school, then got training as a carpenter. In a strange way, the rise and fall of his voice reassured her that things had turned out well for the boy in the story.

Eventually, she moved closer to her bedroom door, letting the conversation downstairs become a backdrop.

Then she moved to a nook in the breakfast room, flicking on a small lamp in the dark corner.

She didn't consider it eavesdropping, because she could only hear the occasional word. It was the cadence of the three male voices—Samuel, Anthony and Luc—that she found comforting while the danger increased for the characters at the story's climax.

"Heather?"

She jumped at the deep voice so close to her. The criminals had now been caught, and she was into the payoff scene at the end of the book.

"Sorry," Samuel rumbled. "Didn't mean to scare you."

"Hi," she said softly, closing the book and setting it down on the table.

He glanced at the title and grinned. "Good story?"

She nodded. Then she shook her head, looking deep into his dark, unfathomable eyes. "How much is…" She bit her bottom lip. "I am *so* sorry for what you went through."

His smile turned sad. "It was a long time ago."

She came up on her knees on the padded bench seat, making her almost eye level with him. Then she put a hand on his bicep. "It must have been horrible for you."

He shrugged his big shoulders. "It was no picnic."

Guilt nipped at her. Her teenage years had been full of designer clothes, sports cars and the right parties. She'd known she was lucky, but she hadn't realized the full extent of her good fortune. She felt her eyes go liquid with sympathy.

"Hey." Samuel tipped her chin up with his index finger. "Is there a soft heart under all that sarcasm?"

She blinked and shook her head. "No."

"Good."

"Good?"

"I like my women tough."

The sheen of tears evaporated completely. "*Your* women?"

He nodded, moving his big palm along her cheek to cup her face, sending reaction sizzling up her spine. "Don't pretend you don't feel it, too." He paused for a moment. "Anthony tells me you're leaving tomorrow."

She nodded jerkily. "I'm taking Joan to Paris."

He shifted forward, crowding her space, leaning in and tipping his head to one side. "Then I guess this is my last chance."

Last chance? "To kiss me?"

His lips curved into a lazy smile, and reflected light shone from his dark eyes. "For starters," he drawled, and Heather's pulse pounded in her ears.

"Then," he continued, "I'm going to show you things your white-bread Boston boys don't even dream about."

She put on a show of bravado. "You think?"

His smile widened meaningfully. "I know."

She couldn't let him get away with this. She was nobody's sex toy—no matter how rawly sensual he appeared. No matter how many erotic dreams he had spawned. And no matter how curious she'd become.

She opened her mouth to tell him so, but he moved in even closer.

His face was mere inches from hers, and she inhaled his woodsy scent. No designer cologne for this man. Her nose twitched at the unfamiliar sensation of real sweat and unadulterated pheromones.

His thumb stroked her cheek, and his lips brushed hers ever so gently. It wasn't a kiss. It wasn't anything, really.

"Only one night," he sighed. "Such a shame."

She was still wearing a pair of fleece shorts and a thin tank top after the heat of the day. A breeze wafted through the window screens and sensitized her bare skin. The scent of hydrangeas filled the air, but the scent of Samuel was stronger.

He brushed a first kiss across her lips, and she thought her legs might give way. "My place," he whispered.

"I can't do that." But she was kissing him back, brushing the tips of her breasts against his chest.

His fingers settled at her waist, finding a thin strip of skin between the elastic of her shorts and the hem of her tank top. "Sure you can." He held back enough to keep the kisses gentle, nearly driving her mad.

"I don't even know you."

His hand crept slowly beneath her shirt. "So what?"

It grazed the underside of her bare breast, and she sucked in a breath. "You could be..."

He flicked his thumb across her nipple. "Dangerous?"

"Yes," she hissed, arching her spine.

"Oh, I'm definitely dangerous." He did it again, and fiery sparks shot the length of her body, leaving a pulsing glow behind them. "And I'm going to have you." He kissed her properly this time. Finally.

His lips overwhelmed hers, plenty of pressure and just the right suction. His tongue curled in, and she opened wide for him, arousal saturating her body.

Then he drew back too soon, the pad of his thumb now

circling her hard, sensitized nipple. His eyes were black, shimmering with knowledge. "It's just a matter of where."

She wanted to argue with him. *Nobody* talked to her that way. Men treated her with respect and deference.

Trouble was, he wasn't only dangerous, he was right. Another five minutes, and they'd be making love on the kitchen floor. Even with her fading rational thought, she knew Samuel's place was a much better choice.

But she couldn't let him have it all his way. She settled her hands on his shoulders, leaned forward from her kneeling position and kissed him this time. Another proper kiss. Another lingering, deep, moist, mobile kiss.

"And if I say yes?"

She felt him smile.

"Have I said anything to indicate you have a choice?"

"I don't think I like where this is leading."

His fingertips feathered up the inside of her bare thigh. Her knees widened reflexively on the cushioned seat.

"Oh, yes, you do." He passed the hem of her loose shorts.

Her hands gripped his shoulders as she lost track of the conversation. She expected him to stop, but his fingers kept on going, past her shorts, past her panties, to slip inside, until he was buried, all but lifting her from the seat.

"My place," he said.

She didn't answer, but then it wasn't really a question.

He kissed her one more time, then scooped her up in his arms and carried her to his truck. She spared a brief thought for what Joan, Anthony or Luc might think, but Samuel's strong arms, erotic scent and whispered demands blotted out the rest of the world.

On the short drive to his place, she watched his profile in fascination. He was a gorgeous man. There was a strength to his features, a wildness that reminded her of the pioneers and conquerors of the dense Louisiana bush. His ancestors hadn't had an easy time of it. But then neither had Samuel.

Perhaps his strength was part lineage, part experience. Whatever it was, it was all sexy, and their midnight tryst had the feel of inevitability.

Then, without warning, Samuel hit the brakes. "Shit!"

Heather glanced frantically out the windshield, her hand shooting out to brace against the dashboard. "What?"

"There's a light."

"A what?"

"In my house." He killed the truck lights, shut off the engine and brought it to a smooth halt.

"Maybe you left it on." She peered at the front of his white cottage. It was prettier and more feminine than she'd imagined.

"I didn't leave it on." There was absolutely no uncertainty in his tone. "You wait here."

Could it be another burglary? Another fan? Another souvenir seeker? "You should call the police."

"I'll be careful."

"Samuel." She didn't want him going into that house. Something was strange in all this, and her instincts hummed.

But he opened his door and stepped out quickly, pushing it shut so that the dome light went off.

He started down the driveway, and Heather sat forward, holding her breath in the darkness. Samuel was a big man, she told herself. He was strong, and he was capable. He'd easily be a match for whoever was in the house. And maybe then they could put an end to all this.

Not that it mattered to her. She and Joan were going to Paris in the morning. But Samuel would still be here. She felt a little funny about that, but she didn't know why.

Samuel was halfway down the walk when the front door burst open. He broke into a run, but then a gunshot cracked the night air, an orange flash shooting out from the porch.

Heather screamed, and Samuel went down.

The shadowy figure vaulted the railing and took off, running through the neighboring yards.

Heather raced to Samuel, screaming his name.

She dropped down on the grass beside him. "Samuel?"

He moaned, and she could see a blood stain spreading from his shoulder down across his chest.

"Cell phone," she cried, knowing she'd left hers at Luc's.

"Pocket," he panted, and she searched the front of his pants.

"Don't you die on me," she pleaded, as she fumbled to retrieve the phone. But she heard a siren in the distance. Obviously the neighbors had called the police.

Thank God.

She leaned over Samuel, grabbing his hand and holding it tightly between both of hers. "Please, don't die." Her voice cracked. "Just don't die."

He didn't answer.

She smoothed his hair back and he grimaced in pain. "Live," she pleaded. "I'll do anything you want. Any position, any kinky perverted thing you can dream up. I promise."

His chest heaved up and down, and she feared it was his last breath. "You're—" he rasped.

She leaned closer, holding his hand against her breasts, fear coursing though her body. "What?"

"You're…going to be…sorry."

"Why?"

"I'm…not…dying."

CHAPTER EIGHT

JOAN KNEW she had to apologize to Anthony. She'd put it off all day, vacillating between anger at his attitude and regret over her own thoughtless words. She'd rather not face him, but she was leaving for Paris in less than twelve hours, and there was no way she could let their relationship end on such a vicious note.

Near midnight, she screwed up her courage and padded down the staircase to the second floor. Anthony's was the room closest to the stairs, next to Heather's closed door.

Joan rapped softly.

"Yeah?" came the gruff reply.

She swallowed. "Anthony?"

There was a silent pause, and she feared he was going to send her away.

"Come in," he finally said.

She slowly pushed open the door. He was propped up in bed, bare-chested, the pages of a manuscript piled on the covers around him.

"Hi," she muttered, and slipped inside.

"Everything okay?" he asked in a cool, professional voice.

She nodded. Then she shook her head. "No, it's not. I am *so* sorry."

He shrugged, but even in the dim light from the bed-side lamp, she could see the distance in his eyes.

"Anthony."

He looked back down at the page. "Don't worry about it."

She took a few steps forward. "But I *am* worried about it. I insulted you, and I insulted your family."

He looked up sharply. "You think *that's* why I'm mad?"

She faltered, confused. "Yeah…"

"I'm mad because you slammed yourself."

She blinked at him.

"Do you honestly think only 'trailer trash' read your books?"

She didn't have an answer for that one. "I…"

He flipped back the covers, and she tensed, afraid he might be naked. But he was wearing boxers.

"They have you brainwashed," he said, coming toward her.

"I can't do this right now," she protested, her throat thickening. She'd come here to apologize, not to fight. She was heartsick at leaving him and heartsick at leaving her career, truth be told. More than at any other time in her life, she needed Anthony's shoulders to lean on.

He took in her expression, and the chill left his eyes. He moved forward and gently pulled her into his arms. "It's going to be okay."

Her chest tightened, and she hiccupped, unable to speak.

"Don't worry," he said, rocking her back and forth.

"I'm so sorry," she mumbled against him. She was sorry for insulting his family, sorry she couldn't be what he wanted her to be, sorry she was leaving him.

She looked up into his eyes, memorizing their intelligence, their sympathy, their passion.

He lifted a hand and brushed her hair back from her temple, sending a familiar wave of desire through her body.

She wouldn't ask. Couldn't ask. After being turned down, a woman didn't beg twice. She had some pride.

The seconds ticked by, and her body molded itself more tightly against his. His scent teased her, and the texture of his fingertips burned into her skin. Her core temperature rose, and her hormones swirled to life until the world contracted to the two of them.

But she wouldn't ask. She…would…not…ask.

"Please?" the whisper slipped from her. "Oh, Anthony, please."

HER WORDS raked over Anthony's soul. Powerless to resist, he swooped down to kiss her mouth. She was delicious, gorgeous in her sleep-disheveled state—an arousing, erotic goddess.

The kiss went on and on. Her lips parted and her tongue met his, hesitantly at first, then with more confidence as his hands roamed up her back, slipping over the thin silk of her robe.

"I've missed you," he groaned.

He didn't ever want to experience her anger or her distance again. If she was going to Paris, so be it. He would take her as Joan Bateman, as Jules Burrell, or as anyone else she wanted to be. If he had to fly to Paris to see her, he'd fly to Paris to see her.

They finally broke the kiss, and she gazed up at him, her round, emerald eyes shinning in the lamplight. "I could come back."

He shook his head sadly. He knew deep down that this was the end. Her family was too powerful, they had too much influence over her. "You won't come back anytime soon."

She didn't deny it.

"I shouldn't have walked away last night," he told her. "I should have dragged you into that bed and made love to you until neither of us could see straight."

She paused, her voice soft. "And now?"

He smiled at her hesitance. He wasn't feeling the least bit unsure. "I like to think I learn from my mistakes."

She smiled, reaching for her robe. "Good."

He followed the movements of her delicate fingers as they worked their way through the knot in her sash. The temperature in the room spiked, and her perfume, her delectable, familiar perfume, wrapped around him in a wave.

He reached for the free ends of her sash and drew her against him. Her hair was loose, and he kissed it tenderly, inhaling deep, mouthing the softness. Then he kissed her forehead, the tip of her nose, and worked his way back to her lips.

With a moan of surrender, she twined her arms around his neck. Her body came flush against his, and all the sensations from the night before rushed back. She was soft where a woman should be soft, narrow where a woman should be narrow. Her hair was fragrant, her skin smooth as warm silk, and deep in her eyes he could see peace and paradise.

He lifted her from the floor, continuing with a kiss that felt bittersweet. It was Joan, finally, and he was losing her in the morning.

The satin of her nightgown slipped against his bare chest. He drew her head into the crook of his shoulder, stroking her soft hair. "I need you," he whispered honestly, rocking her against his body.

"I need you, too," she confessed, and the world started to spiral out of control.

He took the last few steps to his big bed. There he placed her gently on the sheets, following her down to lie beside her.

Her lacy, satin V-neck revealed the mounds of her creamy breasts. He traced the line of lace and felt her tremble beneath his fingers. Then he dipped beneath the fabric, and she sucked in a breath.

He propped himself up with his elbow. "I've dreamed of you," he told her, staring into eyes that had gone opaque with her arousal. "For years and years, I've dreamed of having you in my arms."

A shy smile curved her lips. "I never thought you noticed me."

He chuckled. "Noticed? It's been a struggle to keep my hands off you. Every time we get together, I lecture myself on appropriate behavior."

"You don't say?" she mumbled, burying her face into his bare shoulder.

"I do say."

She pulled back, and her smile turned coquettish as she dropped one strap of her nightgown.

His gaze feasted on her soft shoulders and her creamy cleavage.

Her eyes turned from jade to smoke as she dropped the other strap. Then she pulled one end of the bow holding her bodice together.

He covered her hand with his. "Let me."

She released the tie, and he slowly drew out the satin strip. The bow melted to nothing, and he loosened the final knot. The ties slipped through the eyelets as he eased the silky fabric apart, revealing her breasts, the smooth curve of her stomach and the dusky triangle at the apex of her legs.

"Gorgeous," he breathed, bending to kiss one breast.

Her hands tangled in his hair as he drew her nipple into the heat of his mouth. She squirmed beneath him, her breathing going shallow.

He moaned her name. Then he kissed his way toward her mouth while his hand closed over her damp breast. His tongue tangled with hers, and his fingertips continued an erotic exploration of her body. He tried to take it slow and gentle, but passion surged through him, desperate and impatient.

He trailed his fingers through her silky down, finding his way to her center. His fingers teased her, making her arch toward him.

She groaned his name, fueling his fire, while her fingers fumbled with the waistband of his boxers. Then her hot mouth came down on his flat nipple, and his arousal jacked up to critical.

"Joan," he moaned, grabbing at his boxers.

There was a sharp clatter in the hall.

Anthony swore. He barely had time to flip one end of the quilt over Joan's naked body, when the door burst open, whacking against the far wall.

"Anthony?" Heather cried.

Anthony turned and stared at her, expecting a quick apology, followed by an even quicker retreat.

But Heather just stood there. "Anthony," she repeated, dragging air in and out of her lungs.

Joan sat up, clutching the quilt to her chest. "What's wrong?"

Heather gripped the doorjamb, her knuckles going white under the pressure. "Samuel's been shot."

THE FIRST PERSON Anthony saw in the hallway of the Indigo clinic was Alain Boudreaux.

He headed straight for the police chief, looking for information. "Is he going to be okay?"

Alain nodded. "Doc says he'll be fine."

Anthony raked a hand through his hair and breathed a sigh of relief. Joan gave Heather a tight hug.

"Do we know what happened?" asked Anthony.

"Burglary," said Alain. "Somebody ransacked the house, and Samuel walked in on it."

"Does this happen often?" asked Anthony. Somebody had broken into Samuel's two days ago. He claimed they took nothing. So was this someone new, or were they back?

"We don't know what's going on," said Alain. "But we're starting an investigation."

"Good."

Joan moved forward, pale as a ghost. "Is it connected to me?"

"We don't know that, ma'am," said Alain.

"But it probably is. Why else—"

Anthony took her hand. "They don't know anything yet."

She closed her mouth and nodded.

Anthony turned back to Alain. "Do we know anything about the shooter?"

"Samuel could only say it was a male Caucasian with graying hair. And Heather didn't get a look at him."

Heather shook her head to confirm Alain's statement. She looked small in the clinic foyer, still dressed in her shorts and a thin tank top. "I was in the truck. All I saw was a flash, and then Anthony fell. The ambulance came, but I lost the phone..." Her voice broke on the last words, and Joan rubbed her shoulder.

Heather sniffed back a tear, rubbing her arms as she started to shiver. "Can I see Samuel yet?"

"Soon, I think," said Alain. "He's in surgery."

Anthony glanced around and scooped a blanket from a housekeeping rack, draping it over Heather's shoulders.

"You're not going to take him to St. Martinville?" Joan asked.

The Indigo facility was just a clinic. The surgical capabilities had to be rudimentary.

"The bullet's lodged in his shoulder," Alain answered. "They considered it safer to take it out here than risk the trip."

"He *can't* die," Heather all but wailed, and Anthony realized how traumatic it must have been for her to witness a shooting.

Looking at Joan's stricken face, Anthony pulled both women against his chest, cradling each in one of his arms. He took in Alain's grim expression and wondered just how far this insanity was going to go.

A doctor appeared through a swinging door at the end of the hall, wearing a blue gown, a paper cap and shoe covers.

Heather tore herself from Anthony's arms and rushed forward. "Is he okay?"

The doctor nodded his head. "He's fine. As gunshots

go, it was a minor wound. He'll be groggy for a while, but you can go see him."

Heather nodded, her shoulders sagging in relief as she headed for the swinging doors.

Anthony's arm tightened on Joan. "This is getting out of hand."

She nodded as Alain and the doctor bowed their heads in conversation.

Anthony pulled his cell phone out of his pocket and punched in Luc's number. He kept his arm around Joan, having no intention of letting her out of his sight. This situation had officially stopped making sense two hours ago. Fan or random burglar, Anthony wasn't taking a chance that the shooter might come after Joan.

Luc picked up.

"Samuel's going to be fine," said Anthony without preamble.

"This is bloody strange," said Luc.

"You got that right," said Anthony. "I'm going to bring the girls home. You got any weapons in the house?"

"There's a rifle and an old twelve-gauge."

"That'll do."

"You need some help with this?"

"Appreciate it."

"You got it."

"Thanks." Anthony snapped the phone shut.

"You're joking," said Joan, blinking up at him.

"Do I look like I'm joking?"

She swallowed. "So you *do* think this is my fault?"

"It's not your fault."

"But you do think it's connected to my book."

"I don't know anything yet."

Joan pulled back, squaring her shoulders. "Samuel got shot because of something I wrote."

"We don't know that."

She trembled slightly. "It's my fault."

"It's not your fault."

Her voice went shrill. "Then whose fault is it?"

Anthony stared hard into her eyes. "The guy with the gun."

Heather reappeared through the swinging doors.

Joan went to her sister, and Alain approached Anthony, handing him a business card.

"My cell number's on the back. If Heather remembers any more details, call me right away."

Anthony pocketed the card. "Heather's leaving for Paris in the morning."

"No, she's not," said Heather, wiping her cheeks with the backs of her hands.

"Be better if she stayed," said Alain.

"Be safer if she left," said Anthony.

"I don't think she's in any danger. My men are at Samuel's house, and I don't think the guy came looking to shoot him. It was a case of wrong place, wrong time."

"It *is* his house."

"That's true. And Clem says it's been trashed pretty thoroughly. I'm betting whatever they came for, they found."

"Well, I'm getting the women out of town anyway," said Anthony.

"I'm not leaving town," said Joan.

"You're going to Paris."

She shook her head. "Not until we figure out who shot Samuel."

"How is your staying going to help?" A small part of Anthony couldn't believe he was arguing *for* Paris. But a bigger part of him was frightened for Joan.

"It's my book. Maybe there's something—"

"No, there's not."

"You can't make me leave."

"Yesterday I couldn't make you stay."

"I'm fickle."

"That's true," said Heather.

They both turned to look at her.

"Well, it is," she affirmed, breaking the tension.

Alain tucked his notebook into his breast pocket, turning his attention to Joan. "If you're going to be in town, I do wish you'd reconsider endorsing the music festival, ma'am."

Joan pointed a finger at Alain. "See? He doesn't think I'm in any danger."

Anthony glared at Alain. "He doesn't know what he's talking about."

"I've had fifteen years in law enforcement," said Alain. "I'd take precautions, but there's no need to panic."

Joan poked Anthony in the chest. "Hear that?"

"Thanks a ton," he said to Alain.

Alain shrugged.

"For that," said Joan, "I will endorse the festival."

Alain tipped his hat. "Thank you, ma'am. That's very generous of you."

"It's my damn books that are ruining Indigo," Joan muttered under her breath. "Not the music festival."

"You're going to Paris," Anthony told her.

ALL THE WAY back to the B and B, Joan insisted she wasn't going to Paris, obviously frustrating Anthony.

"Keep the blinds closed and the lights off," he barked as he moved toward the door of the attic suite. "I'm taking the first shift, and Luc's taking the second."

Heather blinked beside her under the covers in the giant bed. "I feel like we're seven."

"That's because you're acting like you're seven," said Anthony.

Heather stuck her tongue out at him.

"Nice," said Anthony, clicking the door shut as he left.

Joan couldn't help but grin. She didn't blame Anthony for being worried, but she'd given it a lot of thought. The only thing that made sense was a souvenir hunt gone wrong. Even if somebody was mad at her for writing *Bayou Betrayal,* there was no reason to shoot Samuel. And if they meant to harm Joan, they would have been at her place or the B and B, not his.

"Protective guy," said Heather into the dim light.

"You know it," Joan agreed. Usually she kind of liked his protective streak. But this time it was proving inconvenient.

She reached for her sister's hand and gave it a squeeze. "You're okay, right?"

"Now that I know Samuel is okay, yes."

Joan considered Heather's profile, trying to make sense of her relationship with Samuel. Last she'd checked, they didn't like each other.

"So, uh, what *were* you doing at his cottage?" she asked.

Heather gave her lacy pillow a couple of whacks, then propped it against the white wicker headboard. "He was going to give me a tour."

"Why?"

"Because it was in your book."

"So?" Samuel's exact cottage wasn't in her book. It was an amalgamation of his, her own and several other Creole cottages in the area.

"So, I read your book today."

Joan stilled.

Heather grinned. "It was terrific."

Emotion built in Joan's chest until it was hard to breathe. She sat straight up, dragging a fluffy, white pillow into her lap. "Are you just saying that?"

"Does 'just saying that' sound like me?"

"No."

"Well, I'm not just saying that. I liked it. It was…" Heather gazed at the ceiling. "I don't know. It was exciting and sexy and enthralling."

"Enthralling?" That was definitely more validation than Joan had ever hoped for from a member of her family.

"You're a good writer, Joanie."

Joan blinked against a sudden burning in her eyes. "You think Mom and Dad will like it?"

Heather choked out a laugh. "Mom and Dad will hate it."

Joan tried to hide her disappointment.

"Face it," said Heather. "The better you write these things, the more popular you'll become, and the more they'll hate it."

"Aarrgghh!" Joan pulled the pillow over her face.

"You can't win on this."

"I know." Joan's voice was muffled. "I know."

Heather patted her shoulder. "You really should have taken up poetry."

"And write about 'the green grass kissing the

morning dew' for the rest of my natural life? I don't think so."

"Don't talk heresy," said Heather.

Joan looked up. "So you really liked my book?"

"I really liked your book."

Joan sighed in satisfaction. Until this *very* moment, she hadn't realized how much Heather's opinion meant to her.

"But we have to talk about the other thing now," said Heather.

"What other thing?"

Heather tilted her head sideways and leaned in close. "I walked in on you and Anthony."

Oh. *That* other thing. "Well…" Joan started slowly. "I guess, under the circumstances, we forgive you."

Heather gave her a shove on the shoulder.

Joan tried really hard not to think about what Heather must have seen.

"I thought you said you weren't sleeping with him."

"I wasn't. I'm *not*."

"What do you mean, you're not."

"I mean…" Joan stopped herself short, realizing she was about to make the situation worse.

Heather blinked at her for a second. "Oh my God." Her shriek of laughter rang out, and Joan buried her face in the pillow.

Footsteps clattered on the stairs.

Before Joan could get her mind around what was happening, the bedroom door crashed open. Anthony and Luc burst into the room, rifles drawn.

"What?" Joan cried.

"You screamed," Anthony roared, his gaze darting to every corner of the room.

Luc turned his back to Anthony's, pointing his weapon at the French doors.

"That was me," said Heather.

"It's nothing, *nothing*," Joan hastily assured them with a frantic shake of her head.

Both men stopped and stared at them.

"You screamed for nothing?" asked Anthony.

Heather swallowed. "I was…uh…laughing."

They lowered their weapons. Luc shook his head in disgust and left the room.

"Laughing?" asked Anthony, his voice incredulous.

Heather swallowed. "At something Joan said."

If Heather went into details, Joan was absolutely going to die.

"I'm glad you find this all so amusing." Anthony raised his weapon and clicked the safety back on.

"It was Joan's book that was funny," Heather snapped. "Not Samuel getting shot."

"Joan's book isn't funny," said Anthony.

"It's funny that I liked it."

His expression changed, and he glanced at Heather with renewed interest. "You liked it?"

"It's brilliant."

He gave a grunt of satisfaction. "See?" he said to Joan.

"Doesn't mean anyone else is going to change their mind," she retorted.

"You thought Heather would hate it."

"My parents will definitely hate it."

"Gotta go with Joan on this one," said Heather.

Anthony shook his head and set his rifle on the table. "I give up."

He crossed the floor to Joan's side of the bed, looking calmer than he had since he'd heard the news about Samuel. He smoothed her hair with his broad palm, then leaned down to kiss her on the forehead. "You're hopeless."

Heather snickered.

He straightened, looking Joan straight in the eye and sending a shiver right down to her toes. "No more accidental screaming, okay?"

"Okay," she agreed.

He gave a sharp nod of acknowledgment, then grabbed the rifle and headed out the door, clicking it shut behind him.

Heather turned to raise her eyebrows. "Explain to me again how you're not sleeping with him."

CHAPTER NINE

SLEEP WITH Anthony?

This morning, Joan was seriously considering killing Anthony.

How could he have set her up like this?

"Ms. Bateman?" prompted Charlie Long from the other end of the line. His voice was as smooth and melodious on the telephone as it was on the television. "I asked if you'd consider flying to L.A. for Friday's show."

Joan scrambled for an excuse. "I...uh...have to—"

"You'd get top billing," he continued.

She closed her eyes and tried to think clearly. A network talk show was a really bad idea. But Charlie Long seemed like a very nice person, and who wouldn't be flattered to get a call in person?

"I'd like to talk about your book, of course. Maybe take the slant that an injustice has been done to the Kane family. It might help to get the case reopened," he added, sweetening the deal.

Joan hadn't thought of it from that angle. But it made sense. Her appearance on *Charlie Long* might actually help Samuel. And she certainly did owe him after yesterday.

But her mother. Oh, her mother.

"I read *Bayou Betrayal*," said Charlie Long. "Loved it."

"Thank you," said Joan automatically. "And I admire your show, too."

"You *do?*" He sounded genuinely pleased. "So... how about helping out a fellow artist? My producers are putting a lot of pressure on me over this one."

"I hear you," said Joan, with genuine empathy. She knew all about pressure. Then she grew angry at Anthony all over again. How could he have put her in this position?

"What do you say?" asked Charlie.

"I need some time—"

"Afraid I've got to have an answer right now. I'm in makeup, and we're promoting Friday's show today."

He was in makeup. Charlie Long was in makeup before his live network show, chatting with her on the phone. Joan went hot, then cold again.

"Help me out, Joan?"

"Sure." Even as she said the word, she couldn't believe she was doing it.

"Great! You're a trouper. I'll see you on Friday."

The line went dead.

Joan clamped her hand around the phone. Deep down, she knew she should be angry with herself. But Anthony made a much more appealing target.

ANTHONY WAS on his feet at the first knock.

"Anthony?" Joan's voice echoed through the door panel.

"Here!" His voice was hoarse as he grabbed the gun and crossed the bedroom, wrenching open the door, checking both ways down the hallway.

But Joan was alone. She stood hale and hearty, eyes squinting at him, arms crossed over her chest. "That was a low-down, dirty rotten trick you pulled."

Anthony lowered the gun and raked back his messy hair, struggling to get his bearings. He checked both ways down the hall again just to be sure. "Huh?"

She stormed past him into the room. "Charlie *Long?*"

Anthony turned, setting the pistol down on a table and pointing it toward the wall. "Charlie Long what?"

"He *called.*"

Anthony went stone-cold. "He called you?"

"Yes, he called me. Did you know?"

Anthony didn't answer. He'd asked Bo to test the waters. But he never expected Charlie Long to make the call without giving him a heads-up.

"Anthony!" Joan cried.

"It was *before* Samuel got shot."

"That's your excuse."

Not exactly. "It was—"

"You're fired."

For a second, Anthony thought he'd misheard. But Joan's expression left no doubt.

She pointed a finger, her voice all but shaking with emotion. "I mean it, Anthony. I'll go to L.A. and do the show, because I promised—"

"You said yes?" He couldn't believe it.

Her voice went shrill. "That's *so* typical."

"It was just a question." If she'd said yes, why was she firing him?

"It's all about business with you, isn't it? Every second of every day. No matter what's going on—bullets flying, nooners with your clients."

Now that wasn't fair. "We never had a nooner."

She glared at him, and he shut up.

"I must be pretty damn important to have Mr. Long call me himself."

"Of course you're important."

"You knew I wouldn't be able to say no. You *knew* it."

"I didn't—"

"Forget it. You can turn it off now, Anthony. In case you missed it, I'm no longer your client."

"Fine," he said.

"Good," she retorted.

"After L.A.," he qualified.

Like it or not, she needed him in L.A. Charlie Long was the big time. She needed his advice, and she needed his protection. They had a ten-year relationship, and he couldn't turn his instincts off like tap water.

"You are no longer on the payroll," she declared.

"I'm still coming to L.A."

"You are not going to change my mind."

"I never thought I would."

"Suit yourself." She flounced toward the door. "But after that, we are done."

"Your choice," he said, schooling his features, pretending there wasn't a hot knife slicing its way through his guts.

"Joanie?" came Heather's cheerful voice, her running footsteps sounding on the staircase.

Joan took a deep breath and carefully evened out her features. "Up here, Heather." Her voice was unnervingly composed.

Heather appeared in the doorway, followed closely by Samuel.

"That was fast," said Anthony, suppressing his own emotions and checking out Samuel's stark white sling. The man was obviously one tough bastard.

Samuel shrugged his good shoulder. "I told them if I wasn't bleeding to death, I wasn't staying. Nobody tried to stop me."

Anthony guessed not.

Heather strode into the room, either oblivious to or ignoring the undercurrents between Joan and Anthony. She perched on his unmade bed. "Samuel has a theory."

"What kind of a theory?" asked Joan. You'd never know from her tone that their relationship had just crumbled into a thousand pieces.

Samuel leaned against the doorjamb, his gaze seeking out Anthony. "I think we may still be dealing with a fan."

"I'm listening," said Anthony, struggling to focus on Samuel.

She'd fired him. *Fired* him.

"When I first read the book," said Samuel, "I thought a lot of it was true."

Heather stood up and paced across the room in her miniskirt and high heels. "Which got us thinking—"

Samuel jumped back in. "Maybe somebody else thought *all* of it was true."

"I'm not following," said Joan.

"The money." Anthony couldn't bring himself to look at her yet. "In your story, there's money stashed in the walls of Samuel's cottage. Somebody thinks it's really there."

Heather snapped her fingers and pointed at Anthony. "Give the man a gold star."

"But I made that up," Joan argued.

"They don't know that," said Samuel. "And I bet they broke into your house first looking for clues."

"They did steal my research notes," Joan conceded.

"Have you talked to Alain?" asked Anthony.

Samuel shook his head. "Thought I'd run it by you first."

Anthony had to admit there was merit to the theory. And if it was true, Joan was in no danger from the shooter. "So you *were* in the wrong place at the wrong time," he said, parroting Alain's words from last night. His faith in the chief was restored.

"I don't think the guy wanted me dead," Samuel suggested. "It was a panic reaction. I caught him in the act, and he was armed."

"Have you been inside your cottage?" Anthony asked. If any of the wall panels were torn down, they'd know the theory was bang on. Just like in *Bayou Betrayal.*

"Not yet," Samuel told him.

Heather took a small half step in Samuel's direction. "If we can avoid the reporters, we're going over there to look around."

"You want to come with us?" Samuel asked Anthony.

"Yeah," Anthony replied with a nod. "But then we have to head for L.A."

Heather looked at Joan and raised her eyebrows in a question.

"I promised to do *Charlie Long Live,*" Joan explained, carefully avoiding looking at Anthony.

Heather's eyes went wide. "Oh, my God."

"I know," said Joan. "It's not what—"

"We never called Mom." Heather darted for the bedroom door, and Samuel quickly stepped out of her way. "She'll have sent the jet to St. Martinville."

Joan swore as she followed her sister out. Anthony still couldn't get used to hearing that word come out of Joan's mouth.

JOAN'S STOMACH cramped as she followed Heather and the men, slinking past the garage to the back door of Samuel's cottage.

She'd fired Anthony.

She was making a point when she did that, an important point about him undermining her wishes. But she'd half expected him to fight for her. Completely expected him to fight for her. Desperately wanted him to fight for her.

But he hadn't.

And now he was fired.

And she couldn't take that back.

She started up the stairs and realized the others had come to a halt in front of her.

She craned her neck. "What?"

Samuel stepped inside, breaking the bottleneck.

Joan worked her way up next to Heather and froze.

Whoever had broken in wasn't joking around. Closets were wide-open. Desk drawers were yanked off their tracks. And the doors of the entertainment center and kitchen cabinets were pulled halfway off their hinges, their contents spilled across the counters and the floor.

Samuel moved through the kitchen, glass crunching under his feet.

Joan swallowed as she silently followed behind.

If you looked past the destruction, it was obvious Samuel took pride in his surroundings. The living room walls and ceilings were painted a spotless cream, accented with exposed, redwood beams crisscrossing their length. She glimpsed a rich, gold-patterned carpet that covered a terra-cotta tile floor, and a redwood mantel finished off a stone fireplace.

The furniture was big and comfortable. Carved from white pine and covered in deep, muted plaid cushions, the sofa and chairs reflected Samuel's stature.

Thankfully, the furniture at least seemed to be intact. And a giant portrait of Samuel's parents still hung above the mantel. It wasn't much of a consolation, but it was something.

"It looks mostly salvageable," said Anthony, picking his way through the living room, surveying the layer of books, papers and kitchen utensils that covered the floor. He came to the bottom of the staircase and gazed up. After a minute, he put his hand on the rail and started to climb.

Heather hurried after him. "You see any broken panels up there?" she called. "Something on the wall that might…" Her voice trailed away as she disappeared down the upper hallway.

Standing next to Joan, Samuel drew in a huge breath. He glanced down at her. "I gotta tell you, my life was a whole lot simpler before you came along."

"Sorry," Joan whispered, her stomach cramping all over again. Disappointing people. There was no doubt she had a knack for it.

"I could hire someone to clean the mess up for you," she offered. It was the least she could do, since this was pretty much all her fault.

He took a couple more steps into the room, shaking his head. "I have to go through everything myself anyway."

Joan nodded in understanding. "You need to know if anything is missing."

Samuel crouched down and flipped through a discarded photo album. "I doubt there's anything missing."

She glanced around at the destruction. "How could you know that?"

"I don't remember the guy carrying anything."

"Well, we know he didn't find the money." It had seemed like such a good plot twist at the time. Now she wished she'd used something else, *anything* else.

Samuel picked up a cracked picture frame, blew off the dust, and straightened to set it on an oak end table. "I have half a mind to hide some cash in the walls myself. Let them take it and put an end to all this."

"A hundred thousand dollars?"

He turned his head and lifted his eyebrows.

"You have that kind of money?" she asked.

"I live a frugal life."

He'd saved that much money on a carpenter's salary? What was he doing working in Indigo, Louisiana? He should invest in the market, open his own business.

He reached down and picked up another leather-bound album. "Not that I want to blow it on some thief."

"You know, Charlie Long says my stint on his show might reopen the investigation." She wasn't convinced Samuel's father was innocent, but the possibility of looking at the case again might be a small consolation to Samuel.

"Might help me more if you told everybody there wasn't any real money involved."

"That's true," she said with a nod. It wasn't a bad idea. Samuel disentangled a lamp from the debris and straightened the shade. "I was joking. They'd never believe you. In fact, some people would take it as proof the money existed."

"What makes you say that?"

"They'll think you're after it for yourself."

"If I wanted it for myself, I would have stolen it before the book was published."

"Maybe." He paused. "Except that you didn't expect people to ever find out you lived in Indigo."

Wasn't that the truth. She put a hand on his arm. "I really am sorry this turned out so bad for you."

"It's not your fault."

"Sure it is. I wrote the book."

He cocked his head and gazed down at her. "You been beatin' yourself up about this?"

She shrugged.

He cracked a smile. "Well, get over it, kid. Shit happens."

Her eyes suddenly burned. With everything crashing down around their ears, Samuel had it in him to care about her feelings. He was an extraordinary man. She wished she'd taken the time to get to know him before this.

She sighed. "Sometimes I feel like everything I touch turns to crap."

"You're really not much like your sister, are you?"

Joan shook her head. No, she'd never been as capable as Heather.

"She got the confidence, and you got the guilt?"

"Maybe. But it's only because everything she does turns out right."

"That's a laugh," said Samuel.

"You should hear her play the violin."

"It's all an act."

Joan rolled her eyes. "A person can't fake playing the violin."

"They can fake liking the violin."

Joan shook her head. "I don't think so." Passion was what separated average musicians like Joan from great musicians like Heather.

"Heather fakes everything," said Samuel.

Boy, did he have that wrong. "No, she doesn't."

"I think she hates her life."

"Trust me, Samuel. Nobody hates a private jet, five-star hotel suites and first-run Broadway tickets." Heather was vivacious, enthusiastic and happy doing pretty much anything. Joan was often envious.

Samuel's smile turned speculative. "So, have you asked yourself why she's still here? Instead of, say, taking in a Broadway play?"

"Because she wants to get me to Paris."

"Why should she care if you go to Paris?"

Heather hadn't made a secret of it. "Because I'm an embarrassment to the family."

"You think?"

"What else is there to think?"

"No walls broken up here," Heather called from the top of the stairs.

Samuel glanced up. "That she's jealous."

Joan blinked. "Of *what?*"

Samuel just smiled.

"It could still be a treasure hunter," Anthony said as he trotted back down.

At the sight of Anthony, Joan's stomach went tight.

He looked so relaxed, so at ease, so unconcerned that they were never going to see each other again.

"I'm going to announce there isn't any money," she said, striving for the same air of unconcern. "On *Charlie Long*. I'll tell the whole world what's true and what's fiction."

"I told her it wouldn't work," said Samuel.

"You'll only fuel more speculation." Anthony sounded certain.

"I have to do *something*." She'd leave for Paris today if she thought it would help. She'd recall every copy of the book if she could. But it wasn't fair to just sit here and let Samuel's life spiral out of control.

"We could torch the house," Anthony suggested.

"No!" Heather jumped forward. "This is a heritage house. Look at the moldings. Look at the scrollwork—"

"I was joking," said Anthony.

Heather scowled. "It wasn't funny."

"We could do a stakeout," said Samuel. "Lie in wait and catch them when they come back."

Heather stared at him. "What makes you think they're coming back?"

Samuel gave her a cocky grin. "To get the money."

"I'm in," said Heather with a rapid nod.

Joan sighed. "I have to go to L.A."

"That's important, too," said Anthony.

"Right," she said. While Heather helped Samuel fix her sister's screw-up, Joan herself would be sitting in a green room somewhere, contributing to the effort by sipping champagne.

JOAN BATEMAN was destined for greatness.

Anthony could see it. Charlie Long could see it. Even the script girl could see it.

The other two guests scheduled for Friday's show

got bumped, and Charlie finished the complete hour with Joan. Anthony had never admired her more. And he'd never felt like a bigger fool. He'd blown the greatest thing that had ever happened to him.

Charlie thanked and congratulated her. What's more, he took that extra five minutes to chat with her and introduce her around. She was on her way to the top, all right.

Anthony realized he had to find her a new agent before he went back to New York. Off the top of his head, there was Calvin Brick. Of course, he was more of a publicity hound than Anthony. Or Tristan Tremayne. But Tristan was known to sleep with his clients. No way was Anthony pushing Joan toward him when she might be feeling vulnerable.

Adrianna Carmichael had handled plenty of bestsellers, but she had burned some editorial bridges, too. That wouldn't be in Joan's best interest. Scratch her off the list.

His cell phone vibrated in his breast pocket.

While Charlie introduced Joan to the producer, Anthony flipped it open, plugging the opposite ear. "Yeah?"

"Remind me to move you to a corner office," boomed Stephen.

"She was good," said Anthony, watching Joan laugh and exchange small talk. The network headed straight into the six o'clock news, and Anthony had to believe a huge audience would have caught the last few minutes of her interview.

"She was money in the bank," said Stephen.

The studio audience was still on its feet, craning

their necks for a look at her, even though security was trying to usher them into the aisles and out the doors.

"I'll tell her you said so."

"Tell her we're scheduling a book tour."

"I don't think so." Anthony would never be scheduling anything for her ever again. But he wasn't sharing that bit of information with Stephen until it was absolutely necessary.

"You got her on the show," Stephen reminded him.

"And it wasn't easy," Anthony pointed out. In fact, it had come at a very big price.

Joan disengaged herself from the crowd. For a woman who hated publicity, her eyes were shining under the stage lights. But then her gaze caught Anthony's, and the glow disappeared. Her smile faded as she started toward him.

Something slammed into his guts. "Gotta go."

"Wait—"

He shut the phone. "You were very good," he said when she got within earshot. She was behind the curtain now, and the sound of the crowd died down.

She tucked her highlighted hair behind one ear. "Charlie seemed pleased."

"Did he invite you back?"

Her eyes narrowed.

Anthony held up his hands. "Just making conversation."

"No." She headed for the hallway to the green room. "He didn't ask me back."

Anthony sighed and tucked his phone back into his pocket.

She walked gracefully in front of him down the wide hallway, her head high, her shoulders square, and her perfect backside swaying ever so slightly beneath a tight pin-striped skirt and a cropped blazer.

He didn't often see her in high heels, and the sight of her long legs made his pulse pound. It gave him a flashback to their interrupted lovemaking, forcing him to set his jaw and shake off a rush of the inappropriate hormones.

He did a quick step to catch up. "Hungry?" he asked over her shoulder.

She shrugged.

"We have to eat," he persisted, wanting to keep their lines of communication open a little longer, at least until he could get her set up with someone else. "There's a nice seafood place over on Sunset."

And, if he recalled correctly, the restaurant had a great deck overlooking the ocean, and the service was ridiculously slow. They'd have a chance to talk.

"I was thinking I'd head for the airport," she said.

"Our flight's not until tomorrow."

They emerged into the opulent green room, and Joan headed straight for the attendant behind a small desk near the entry. "Could you please call me a taxi?"

The uniformed woman smiled and picked up the telephone. "No need, ma'am. One of our drivers can help you."

"Thank you," said Joan.

"You're going to spend the night at the airport?" The network had given them a huge, three-bedroom hotel suite.

She moved away from the desk, and he followed.

"I'm sure I can find a flight."

"The red-eye?"

"Whatever."

"Joan?" He touched her arm, but she shook him off. "Why are you doing this?" he asked, jockeying around to try to look her in the eye. Surely she didn't want to say goodbye in a studio green room.

She kept her back to him.

"Joan?" he repeated, glancing up at the attendant to make sure they weren't being overheard.

She finally turned, and her eyes looked haunted. "Can't you just let it die?"

"No," he answered honestly. "Can you?"

She glanced away.

After a moment of terse silence, he dragged his hand through his hair. "Is that it, then? We say goodbye *here?*"

Her lips were pursed tight, and she fixed her stare on the far wall.

"You have the greatest moment of your professional career." He tried unsuccessfully to keep his voice from breaking. "And then you walk away from me forever?"

Her tone was bitter. "You think that was the greatest moment of my professional career?"

"It was *Charlie Long.*"

"Ma'am?" queried the attendant.

Joan looked up.

"Your car is out front."

"I'm coming with you," said Anthony.

"No, you're not."

"Is there a problem?" asked the attendant, coming around the small desk to frown at Anthony.

"No problem," said Joan, increasing her pace.

"No problem," Anthony echoed, keeping up.

"Go away," she hissed.

"Not a chance."

"You've been fired."

"Not until we're out of L.A."

Joan stopped abruptly and turned back to the anxious attendant. "Could you please call security?"

Anthony couldn't believe he'd heard right. "Don't be ridicu—"

"This man is bothering me."

CHAPTER TEN

HEATHER CAME to a halt beside Samuel at the bottom of a ladder-like staircase that disappeared into the gloom of the opera house cupola. They'd already explored the dusty, cluttered attic above the stage in their quest for a safe stakeout. Fading light filtered through the cupola windows, adding to the illumination of Samuel's flashlight.

"If you're afraid to climb—" there was a thread of amusement behind his jab "—you can always wait here."

"I'm not afraid," Heather lied, eyeing the steep staircase, working on quelling the butterflies in her stomach. She was pretty sure she could make it to the top. It was getting back down that might kill her.

"You sure?" he asked.

There were numerous windows in the cupola, and Samuel had assured her they'd have a view of his house from three sides. They were armed with a low light camera in the hopes of getting a shot of whoever had broken in. Vertigo or not, Heather wasn't missing out on the action.

"I'm sure," she said, taking a bracing breath.

"Great." His full lips curved into a calculating smile.

"What?" she asked.

His voice turned seductive. "You remember what you promised me?"

"No," she lied, not meeting his eyes, even as her pulse jumped.

"Liar," he purred in her ear.

Of course she was lying. But the promise had been an impulse born of fear. And he hadn't died. And, despite the buzz building in her body, she really wasn't ready for whatever kinky sex thing he had in mind.

She put her foot on the bottom step.

He caught her by the arm. "Not so fast."

"We need to get into position," she said.

His chuckle told her how he'd interpreted her words, while his thumb drew little circles on her bare arm. She was suddenly, acutely conscious of her short, cotton skirt and her tight tank top.

"You know what I meant," she said tartly, attempting to pull away. But a little part of her—okay, a big part of her—wanted him to push a little.

"A promise is a promise," he mocked, as if reading her mind.

"I thought you were dying at the time."

"But I lived."

The silence stretched until she braved a look into his eyes.

Hoo boy.

Those were some sexy eyes. And his thumb was roaming toward her shoulder. Who knew a shoulder could be so arousing?

He didn't say a word, just stared at her while the debate raged inside her head.

"What did you have in mind?" she finally asked, telling herself there was no harm in hearing him out.

Maybe it wasn't something hugely kinky. Maybe it was something normal. Although, if it was too normal, she'd be disappointed.

What was she *saying?*

"Take off your panties," he rumbled.

The butterflies regrouped in her stomach. "Why?"

"Because you promised any kinky perverted thing I could dream up."

Okay, this wasn't looking so normal. "What are you going to do?"

"You'll see."

She shook her head. "Uh-uh."

He nodded. "Uh-huh."

"Not unless you tell—"

"Take them off."

"No."

"Yes."

There was laughter lurking behind his eyes. He was yanking her chain. He wasn't going to do anything awful.

Was he?

"Now," he said.

"Fine." She held up her index finger. "But this better not hurt."

"It won't hurt."

"You promise?"

"Live a little, Heather."

She stared at him for another second, trying to decide if she was being incredibly brave or incredibly stupid. Then she reached under her skirt and hooked her thumbs around her lacy panties, pulling them down and kicking them off over her sandals.

There. She'd promised, and she was following

through. It was the only honorable thing to do. She really had no choice.

He scooped them up and tucked them into his pocket.

She folded her arms over her chest, trying not to let the air currents swirling up against her damp flesh turn her on. "Now what?"

Would he tie her to the railing? Take her up against the attic wall? Had he brought along some kind of sex toy?

"We go upstairs," he said easily, gesturing for her to precede him.

"We're going to have kinky sex on the catwalk?"

"Who said anything about kinky sex?"

"But…" Her jaw dropped open as she realized his intent. "You pervert."

"I think we pretty much established that already."

She bopped him in the chest with the end of her fist. "You're going to look up my skirt."

"Hey, it was your idea in the first place."

"I—"

"And it was a good one."

"And you swore you didn't do that kind of thing."

"Not without permission." He moved closer again. "Can I assume I've got your permission?"

"You may not."

This time, he crossed his arms over his chest. "Never took you for a tease."

"I'm not a tease."

"You sure make promises you won't keep."

"You tricked me."

"I did," he nodded. "That was my master plan all along. Get shot, and get you to promise me kinky sex."

"You're insufferable." It might not have been a setup, but it sure felt like a setup.

"Tell me something, Heather."

"What?"

"Do you *want* to climb up those stairs in front of me?"

His question sent a shiver down her spine. She opened her mouth to tell him no, but his intent gaze told her he'd know she was lying.

Truth was, now that she really thought about it, climbing up those stairs with Samuel behind her would be daring. It would be sexy—like nothing she'd every done before, like nothing she'd ever do again.

"It's just you and me, babe," he rumbled, his rough fingertips brushing a tendril of hair back from her face. "None of your Boston boys will ever have to know."

He had a point.

She lifted her lashes to gaze into his dark, sinful eyes. If she was ever going to go out on a sexual limb, now was the moment to do it. And this moment might never come again. She was more than a little nervous, but she turned away and started up the first steps.

Her skirt swished, and her thighs fanned each other as she walked up one step, then another, then another. She could feel Samuel's gaze, hot and prickly on the backs of her legs.

The aging wood groaned and the staircase bowed as he mounted the first step. She kept climbing, and he kept pace, the distance remaining constant between them.

By the time she stepped out on the catwalk, she was a heated mass of hormones. Her skin gleamed slickly in the fading light. And it was a fight to keep from throwing herself in his arms.

Samuel moved to a floor-level window, removing the camera from around his neck. "This'll work," he said, then eased his big body down to lean back against the wall.

Heather stared at him in disbelief. Where was the kiss? Where was the embrace? Where was the fast, hard sex up again the wall?

"What?" he asked.

She pushed back her damp hair, trying to ignore the throbbing insistence between her legs. "I thought…"

He lifted his brows, his expression deadpan.

She took a step forward. "Then *what the hell* was that all about?"

He grinned. "That was about me watching you walk up a flight of stairs."

"But—"

"You thought we'd have sex now?"

Who wouldn't think they'd have sex now? Wasn't that the point of foreplay? Wasn't that the point of getting her out of her panties and talking dirty?

Unless he didn't want sex. Was there something about the glimpse of her butt that had turned him off?

"Put the insecurity on hold," he said, lifting his sling. "I'm waiting until I have two good arms."

"Oh." They couldn't do it more than once?

He nodded out the window. "And I can't get a picture of our thief if I'm banging you, can I?"

Okay. Fair enough. Now she just felt stupid.

His voice turned gentle. "But come and sit on my lap."

She rolled her eyes. "Will you make up your mind?"

"I have made up my mind. I'm here for a stakeout. But you'll make it more entertaining. Unless you think the bare floor will be more comfortable."

She squinted down at the wooden planks. "I'd probably get splinters."

"You probably would." He held out his good arm.

She moved toward him. "Fine. But you keep your hands to yourself."

He steadied her as she lowered herself into his lap. "Ah, Heather. I'll put my hands anywhere my little heart desires." And then he set his warm, broad palm on the top of her thigh.

"I hate you," she said, wishing he'd take his hand away, but hoping he'd move it higher. She was a pathetic jangle of sexual need, and he had her completely under his spell.

He chuckled. "It's not me you hate. It's that prison you've locked yourself inside."

What a ridiculous statement. "I'm not in a prison."

His fingertip moved ever so slightly, and she sucked in a gasp.

"What should you be doing?" he asked.

"About what?"

"Tonight. It's Friday. If you weren't in Indigo with me, where would you be?"

A pithy swearword zinged across her brain as she realized she'd stood up her date. *Jeffrey Plant.*

"Who's Jeffrey Plant?"

"My date. Back in Boston. I'm supposed to be at the Heidelberg Strings. What time is it?"

"A little past eight."

"Give me your cell phone."

"Please?"

She turned to glare at him. "Please."

"Sir?"

"This isn't about sex."

"Everything's about sex."

"Well, we're not going there."

"Sure we are."

No, they weren't. They were *not*. "I need to call my boyfriend," she lied.

He reached into his pocket and handed her the phone, his expression telling her he guessed she was exaggerating the relationship.

"Thank you," she said, before she realized being polite would only encourage him in his fantasy.

"Sir," he rumbled, as she pushed the buttons.

"Never," she growled back.

"Hello?" came Jeffrey's voice through the small speaker.

"Jeffrey?" She tried to sit forward, but Samuel snaked an arm around her waist and pulled her back into the cradle of his thighs.

"Heather? Where are you?" The sound of a crowd was in the background, and she could picture him in his tuxedo in the lobby of the Wang Center.

Guilt had her struggling in Samuel's grasp, but it was futile. "I'm in Indigo with Joan."

Samuel snorted, and she reached back to bop him.

"You're supposed to be *here*," said Jeffrey.

"I'm sorry…sir," she added to needle Samuel.

In retaliation, his hand moved up and closed over her breast.

She inhaled sharply at the sensations that instantaneously shot through her body.

"I don't like what I'm hearing about your sister," said Jeffrey.

"What are you hearing?" She bit down on her bottom lip in an effort to combat the impact of Samuel's caress.

"What do you mean, what am I hearing? I'm hearing what everybody else is hearing."

Samuel's fingers closed on her hardened nipple.

She swallowed a groan. "It's complicated," she gasped into the phone.

"I don't particularly care if it's complicated. When are you coming home?"

"I don't know."

His voice turned imperious. "Make it now."

Heather didn't remember that tone being so annoying. "I can't."

Samuel's fingers tightened, not quite enough to hurt, but enough to command her total attention.

"Yes, you can."

She pawed at Samuel's hand, but she was no match for his strength. "I have to go, Jeffrey."

"Go where?"

If he knew. If he only knew.

"Bye," she whooshed, and quickly hung up. Then she rounded on Samuel. "That was outrageous!" she sputtered.

He grinned unrepentantly. "That was fun."

"You can't...just...when I'm..."

His palm smoothed over her aching nipple. "You going to tell me you didn't like that?"

She breathed deeply, trying not to get distracted from her anger. "That's not the point."

"It's exactly the point. Whoa." His hand left her breast, and he quickly lifted the camera to his eye.

Heather swung her gaze toward the window. "You see something?"

"Hang on."

She pulled back. "Should I move?"

"You're fine."

She focused on the tiny figure moving through Samuel's backyard. The shutter clicked in her ear as Samuel took pictures of the person making his way toward the porch.

"Should we go grab him?" she whispered.

"I don't want any more shooting," said Samuel. He clicked the shutter a few more times.

"Are the pictures any good?"

"Not yet. I'm just getting the back of his head."

"Where's he—" The man kept on going right past the porch.

Samuel lowered the camera from his eye. "Maybe it's not him."

"Then what's he doing in your yard?"

"I don't know."

The man disappeared into a copse of trees. "Where'd he go?"

"The tool shed's down that trail. There."

The figure reappeared, jiggling the catch on the wooden door.

"He won't find anything in there," said Samuel. "Nobody's been in it for years."

While they watched, the man gave up on the door and walked down the side of the shed. At the back corner, he look furtively around and then dropped to his knees.

"What on earth?" Heather breathed.

Samuel put the telephoto lens back up to his eye. "He's digging."

"For what?"

"Now, that's gotta be the long shot of the century."

"Buried treasure?" asked Heather.

"Is he going to check every square inch of my yard?" They watched for a few more minutes.

"Should we call Alain?" she asked.

"Yeah." Samuel tossed her the phone again.

"Maybe he's crazy?" she offered as she glanced down at the lighted number pad.

"I'd say that was a safe—" Samuel froze.

"What?"

"He's... Son of a bitch!" Samuel all but shoved her off his lap. He jumped to his feet and bailed down the long staircase.

JOAN STUFFED her clothes into the suitcase that was open on the high, four-poster bed in the opulent hotel suite provided by the network. Too bad she wasn't going to be able to stick around and enjoy the amenities. It had been years since she'd lounged in a whirlpool bath, sipping champagne and gazing out at the lights of a beautiful city.

But right now, it was more important to get out of L.A. and back to Indigo. She was holding herself together by a thread around Anthony, second-guessing her decision, inches away from begging him to take her back. She needed to cut the cord and get completely away from him.

He was a publicity maniac, she told herself. Their approaches to her career were in complete opposition to each other. The fact that he was funny and smart and sexy, and that she had an unfilled sexual ache for his body had no bearing whatsoever on her professional decision.

He muddled her thinking, and she needed to get away from him as soon as humanly possible.

She slammed the suitcase shut and pushed the catches closed.

"Joan?" Anthony's voice sounded from the entry hall, and her heart sank.

She'd told him she was going straight to the airport in the hopes he'd waste time scouring LAX. Her plan had been to make a quick stop at the hotel and then take a cab to Ontario Airport. She could get a flight to New Orleans from there.

"Joan?" he called again, his voice getting closer as he made his way down the hall.

There was a slim chance she could cut through the bathroom and evade him.

"Joan?"

So much for that.

He strode through the bedroom doorway. "You tried to have me *arrested?*"

She didn't look up. "I was trying to get you to back off." Why, oh, why couldn't he take a hint?

He was quiet for a strained moment and the muted sounds of traffic wafted through the windows.

"So, this is really it?" he asked.

Of course it was it. She thought she'd made that pretty plain. She finally looked up. "What were you expecting?" Her hand tightened on the suitcase handle, and she heaved the bag off the bed.

He leaned forward and tried to take it from her.

She shook her head, pulling back. "I'm fine."

"It looks pretty heavy."

"I've been carrying my own suitcase most of my life." Why couldn't he just go away?

He waited patiently until she finally met his eyes.

His blue ones burned into hers, and it was impossible to miss the hurt and confusion in their depths.

She felt terrible hurting him. He was her friend.

He'd stood by her side for ten years. Sure, his ideals were different from hers. But until *Charlie Long Live,* he'd never deliberately undermined her. Maybe she hadn't given him enough time to explain. Maybe…

While she argued with herself, something shifted in his expression. His eyes swirled to cobalt, and her hormones answered. Her pulse spiked in reaction, causing sweat to gather on her palms and form between her breasts.

"I can't believe you're going to let it end like this," he whispered, shifting forward, his husky voice adding to the confusion in her body.

"It's already over," she rasped.

"Can we at least say goodbye like civilized adults?"

She swallowed, her pulse rate erratic beneath her tingling skin. "Goodbye, Anthony."

He took two final steps, and he was right in front of her, forcing her to look up at him.

"Goodbye, Joan." He smiled sadly. "You have been…" As his voice faded, he leaned ever so slightly toward her.

His scent surrounded her, and her wild pulse pounded in her ears. Her suitcase handle grew slick against her palm.

His voice dropped even further, "…*the* greatest experience of my life."

The suitcase slipped from her fingers to topple on the rug.

"Anthony," she sighed, abandoning her iron control, fixating on his lips, remembering every second of every kiss they'd ever shared.

He bent toward her. "I'll miss you, Joan Bateman."

She felt tears burn the backs of her eyes. "I'll miss you—"

But then his lips touched hers. So soft, so sweet, so hot.

Their mouths fused, opening in unison, so their tongues tangled together. His hands cradled her face, and her arms wound around his neck.

It might have been meant as a goodbye kiss, but it instantly turned into something else altogether.

He stepped into the embrace, his hard body coming flush against hers. She moved against him, fisting her hands and digging them into the back of his neck. She pressed closer, closer, closer still.

She couldn't let him go. This one moment in time had to last forever, because when it was over, he was walking out of her life for good. He was fired, and she was alone.

"So sweet," he muttered against her lips. His hands smoothed down her sides, then rounded to the small of her back. "So beautiful. You are the sexiest woman alive."

She wanted him.

She wanted him more than she'd ever wanted anything in her life, more than saving Indigo, more than publishing a book, more than appeasing her family. She wanted Anthony here and now, naked and inside her, even if she regretted it every second of every day for the rest of her life.

Something vibrated against her shoulder.

She jumped back. "What on—"

"My phone," he mumbled, recapturing her lips and kissing her again.

It vibrated a second time, tickling her.

"Damn." He ripped it out of his pocket and threw it on the bed.

"You should answer it," she said around his next kiss. Real life was still out there, whether she wanted it to be or not.

"Screw it." He kissed her neck.

The sixth muffled buzz sounded from the bed.

"Anthony."

He sucked in a harsh breath and reached down to grab the phone. He flipped it open, his voice a bark. "Yeah?"

He was silent for a moment.

Then he blinked and gave his head a little shake. "I don't—"

More silence.

Joan felt a chill. The regret she'd fully expected was upon her—even sooner than she'd feared. She started for her suitcase, but his hand shot out, grabbing her arm to stop her.

"I agree," he said into the phone, giving her a look that clearly ordered her to stay put. Not that she could break the grip on her arm. Not that she wanted to. She should want to, she knew. But she didn't. And there it was.

"Okay," said Anthony. "Maybe Dallas for a few days."

Business. He had already moved on. Something inside her died a whimpering death.

"Talk to you then," he said and flipped the phone shut.

He stared down at her for a heartbeat, the earlier passion completely erased from his eyes. "We have a problem."

She squared her shoulders. If he could move on, so could she. "What kind of a problem?"

His grip had loosened on her arm, so she reached for her suitcase.

"That was Samuel," he said.

Joan stopped, her fear turning to Heather. "What's wrong?"

"He thinks…" Anthony tucked the phone back into his pocket. "He saw someone dig up a baseball bat in his backyard."

Joan squinted at Anthony. "So what?"

"The police thought his mother was hit with a baseball bat before she was shot. But they never found it."

Joan nodded. "Okay. Yeah. I read that in the transcript."

"If this is the baseball bat…"

A shiver of true fear ran through Joan. If this was the same baseball bat, there was only one person who would know where it was. "Then there really is a murderer out there."

"And your book has made him nervous."

She shook her head, taking an involuntary step back. "It's not possible. I made it all up."

"We can't take that chance."

"What do we do?"

"We go to Dallas for a few days. If Samuel's right, you can't be in Indigo right now."

"But what about Samuel? What about *Heather?*"

"You're the one the person's scared of."

"But I don't know anything." The whole situation took on a brand-new feeling of unreality.

"Samuel's talking to Alain. Let's give the police department a few days. We can stay with my parents until then."

Stay with Anthony's parents? With *Anthony?* With

all that was going on between them? Bad idea. Really, really bad idea.

"I can go to Boston," she said, even though she dreaded facing her own parents.

He stared down at her, looking all protective and Anthony again. She tried hard not to treasure that look.

"You honestly think there's a chance in hell I'm going to let you out of my sight?"

"I fired you." Her voice cracked over the words.

"We're in this together, Joan. *Together.*"

CHAPTER ELEVEN

JOAN AND ANTHONY headed straight for the airport after Samuel's call. They managed to catch a red-cye to Houston, then they hopped an afternoon flight to Dallas and rented a car. By the time they pulled into his parents' driveway, Joan was exhausted and a nervous wreck.

She fluffed her hair, checking the visor mirror to make sure her makeup wasn't too badly smeared.

"You sure this is going to be okay?" she asked for the hundredth time.

"They're thrilled," he reassured her. "I haven't been home in nearly a year."

"I know they're happy to see you. It's me that might be the problem."

He slanted her a look of frustration as he shut off the key. "They're friendly people, Joan."

"But I'm an uninvited guest."

"Stop it."

"Stop what?"

He opened the driver's door. "Let's go."

Joan took a deep breath. If Anthony's family seemed at all uncomfortable, she'd go to a hotel. In fact, she'd suggested that to Anthony already. But he'd said his mother would be offended and might never speak to him again if they dared even suggest hotel rooms.

She stepped gingerly onto the concrete driveway and glanced around.

They were in an older, but very well-maintained family neighborhood. The lawns were lush, the hedges trimmed, and the driveways wound through generous sized lots to multi-story houses of brick and stone.

The Verduns' house had a wide, front porch, with square pillars supporting the roof and double front doors, bracketed with sidelight windows. A rustic, willow furniture grouping on the porch looked like an inviting spot to spend a cool, fall evening.

She followed Anthony up the semicircular stairs, wondering how much he'd told them about her. Did they know she was a client? Did they think she was a friend?

As they stepped onto the porch, the double doors burst open. "Anthony!" A sixtyish woman burst through the entrance and pulled him into a warm hug.

"Hey, Mom." Anthony responded by wrapping his arms around her and lifting her slightly off the ground.

Then he put her down, kept one arm around her and gestured to Joan. "This is Joan Bateman."

"Joan!" The short-haired, rounded woman rushed forward again, this time wrapping Joan in an enveloping hug that lasted about five seconds too long for Joan's comfort zone.

The woman finally released her. "Such a delight to meet you."

"I'm happy to meet you, too," said Joan, with a backward step.

Anthony immediately swooped in and put a hand on the small of her back. "Watch the stairs behind you."

Joan stilled. "Right."

She focused on Anthony's mother. "I hope this isn't an imposition."

The woman smiled broadly and waved away her concern. "Nonsense. We're thrilled to have you." She smoothed her mint-green cotton blouse over her khaki shorts. "I'm Anna. Anthony's father, Oscar, is in back in the yard. The—"

"Anthony!" Another body burst through the doors. A younger woman in denim shorts, flip-flop sandals and a blue-and-white striped tank top launched herself into Anthony's arms.

Joan surreptitiously braced herself on the railing, just in case she was next.

"This is Nadine," said Anna. "She's Anthony's brother Brett's wife."

The lithe and tanned Nadine pulled away from Anthony and tucked her long, dark hair behind her ears. She turned and stuck out her hand to Joan. "You must be Joan."

Joan breathed a sigh of relief as she shook the woman's hand. "Yes. Joan Bateman."

Just then, a man who looked remarkably like Anthony appeared. "About time you showed up," he boomed to Anthony with a hearty, backslapping handshake.

"And this is Brett," said Anna.

Nadine took in Joan's expression, then leaned forward to whisper conspiratorially, "I was new once, too. Don't let them intimidate you."

"Thanks," said Joan, wondering how far it was to the nearest hotel.

"Let's not stand around our here on the porch," said Anna, ushering them toward the door with expansive arm gestures. "Dad's got the grill going."

Joan followed Anthony and his slightly larger brother.

"Carlos is playing a gig in Amarillo," said Anna as they made their way through a gold-and-tan-colored foyer, cluttered with shoes, tennis rackets and a guitar leaning up against the wall.

The living room looked well used, with worn, over-stuffed leather furniture, a massive stone fireplace, plants on every conceivable surface, and magazines piled haphazardly from the floor to a crowded bookcase. Obviously, Anna hadn't been expecting company this weekend.

They cut through the kitchen. High-ceilinged, and done in the same muted gold and earth tones, it seemed more organized than the other rooms.

There was a hint of freshly baked cookies in the air, and appliances of every description covered the granite counters. Two wine racks were cut into the stone of a feature wall. Wrought-iron chairs were lined up beside a breakfast bar, and Joan could easily picture family members chatting with Anna while she cooked.

"David's family should be here soon," sang Anna as she opened French doors leading to a huge cedar deck. It was obvious the family spent a lot of time outside.

"David is the youngest," Nadine offered. "He has three little kids, and his wife, Leila, hasn't slept through the night in years."

"Do you have any children?" asked Joan.

Nadine shook her head. "I teach third grade. So far, I haven't had the desire to go 24/7 with the little mites."

Joan smiled. Her own experiences with children were few and far between. She hadn't decided about them one way or the other. Not that she was in a position to become a mother anytime soon.

"Joan?" called Anna from the other side of the deck. "This is Oscar, Anthony's father."

A big, burly man, wearing a Kiss The Cook apron and brandishing a spatula, descended on Joan.

Her mind barely had time to register panic before she was enveloped in a hug. She tensed for a second, but then realized his arms were gentle, his voice soft and teasing, and his scent a pleasant mixture of tangy spices.

"Welcome to Texas," he rumbled against her.

"Thank you," she managed as he pulled away.

"Anthony gives you any trouble, you come to me," he winked.

"Anthony's given me plenty of trouble," she joked under her breath, feeling relieved by his jovial manner.

Oscar waved the spatula in Anthony's direction. "You behave yourself."

Anthony held up his hands. "Whatever she told you, it wasn't me."

Everyone laughed.

Oscar turned back to Joan. "How do you like your burgers?"

"However you're cooking them will be fine."

He ruffled her hair. "That's my girl." Then he called back to Anthony. "Don't you let this one get away."

Joan kept the smile pasted on her face, but didn't dare look at Anthony.

"Can I get you a drink?" asked Nadine.

"Please," said Joan without a second's hesitation.

"Anything in particular?"

"Strong." Joan wasn't feeling choosy at the moment.

"David!" cried Anna, bustling toward the kitchen door. "You made it."

The deck was instantly a whirl of toddlers.

"They drove down from Oklahoma City," said Nadine. "Come on. The margarita machine is this way."

"It looks a little crowded around here," Joan said to Nadine. If David and his family were staying over, Anna was going to have a houseful. "Have we come at a bad time?"

"What? No. We're all here to see you."

Nadine led Joan over to an electric drink machine that was churning a lime-green mixture in a glass cylinder.

"They came all that way to see Anthony?" asked Joan. Now *that* was a loyal family.

Nadine handed her a plastic cup of margarita mixture. "Not Anthony. *You.* Anna called to tell us y'all were coming, so we dropped everything."

"I don't understand," said Joan, giving her head a little shake.

"We love your books. Well, we love Anthony, too. But we *really* love your books."

"You've read *Bayou Betrayal?*"

"We've read them all. Of course. We thought they were written by a man."

It took a second for the words to sink in. "You've read them *all?*"

Nadine lifted her own drink to her lips, nodding. "Sure did. Me and everybody else."

"You mean to tell me your family reads all of Anthony's clients' books?" He'd told her he had a supportive family, but that was way beyond the call of duty.

Nadine grinned and shook her head. "We didn't know you were Anthony's client."

Now that was even stranger. "Then why?"

"Because they're great stories. You do realize you'll

have to sign about sixty copies before we'll let you out of here, don't you?"

"I'll sign anything you want." Joan glanced around the deck in astonishment. These people had all read her books?

"Loved *Black Nights on Water*."

Joan smiled at Nadine with genuine pleasure. "It was a fast write. I loved playing around with the Joe McIntosh character."

"He was hot," Nadine agreed. "Saw you on *Charlie Long* last night. You're a natural."

Joan's smile faltered. "I'm not crazy about the publicity." She didn't mention the situation with her family. Judging by what she'd seen of the Verduns so far, Nadine probably wouldn't understand.

"Could've fooled me."

"I don't think I'll do any more of it."

"No way. Really?"

Joan nodded. "I just want to write books." Though even that was up in the air at the moment.

"But you could be famous."

Joan chuckled and took a deep drink of the icy margarita. "I wouldn't go that far."

"I would. So, what was he like?"

"Anthony?"

Nadine snorted. "Charlie Long."

"Oh. Really nice. Surprisingly nice."

"Did you get an autograph?"

"Never thought of it."

"Hi, y'all." A soft-spoken young woman, about five feet two, with a toddler on her hip, joined the conversation.

"Joan, this is Leila, David's wife."

"I guessed that by the little one," said Joan, reaching out to shake Leila's hand. She hardly looked strong enough to carry the child.

"Margarita?" asked Nadine.

"You bet." The toddler squirmed and whined, and Leila put him down. "Watch him near the edge," she called to a man who had to be David.

She smiled hesitantly at Joan. "David told me not to ask you this."

Joan tensed. Had they heard she'd fired Anthony? "What?" she asked slowly.

Nadine handed Leila a margarita, and Leila took a large swig.

"Anthony just sold my first book."

"He did?"

"A suspense novel."

"Congratulations!" Joan was delighted to share in such happy news. She remembered her first sale vividly. The first one was Brian's, of course. But the second one, the one she'd done all on her own, had been a momentous occasion. Anthony had taken her out to lunch, since she couldn't tell anyone else about it.

For the first time, she felt a tinge of sadness at the memory.

Leila was nodding, her eyes focused on her orange plastic glass as she ran a fingertip around the rim. "I'm not supposed to…" She glanced furtively back at her husband. "Would you read it? And maybe give me a quote? Only if you like it. Only if you…" She clamped her mouth closed.

"Of course I will," said Joan. "But I don't know how a quote would help you."

"We'd put it on the cover."

"But I'm…nobody special."

"Are you kidding?"

Joan took another drink. "Really. You guys. You're embarrassing me."

She felt an arm across her back. Even with all the hugging in this family, she instinctively knew it was Anthony.

"Everything okay?" he asked.

"We're getting her drunk," said Nadine.

He nodded toward Joan's margarita. "You be careful of those."

Joan took a defiant swig. "It's a good day to get drunk." It was.

She was suddenly happy to be here. Anthony's house was a great place to hide out emotionally for a while. Her parents were far away. Indigo was far away. Anthony was still her agent for a couple more days. And his family liked her books.

That was a very nice thing to hear.

She held her glass out to Nadine. "Can I have another?"

Nadine took the glass with a grin.

"Don't say I didn't warn you," said Anthony.

"I'm a big girl," said Joan, with a toss of her hair. A few strands caught on his face, and he brushed them away, smoothing a hand over her scalp.

"And you can take care of yourself," he mumbled.

It was probably a dig, but she chose to ignore it. "Absolutely."

ANTHONY'S BROTHER Brett eased himself down in the next lawn chair, parked his beer on the grass and settled his second, loaded burger on a paper plate in his lap.

"So, what's the deal?" he asked Anthony now that they had a moment alone.

"The deal?" Anthony took a sip of his own beer. He'd gone with a Bud Light. He figured Joan was drinking enough for both of them.

"You've been Jules Burrell's agent all these years, and you didn't say anything?"

Anthony slanted his brother a look of disbelief. "You're joking, right?"

"Hey, we're family."

"So I should risk getting disbarred to share gossip?"

It was Brett's turn to shrug. "I'm just saying, you could have hinted."

Anthony snorted.

"She's a woman," said Brett.

"She is," Anthony agreed.

"A hot woman."

Anthony didn't answer.

"Don't you think?"

Anthony's gaze strayed to where Joan was laughing with Nadine. Not that he hadn't been watching her most of the evening anyway. "I'm not blind."

"And you brought her here."

"Yeah."

"That means something's going on between you."

"No. That means things are uncomfortable for her in Indigo right now."

"You could have taken her anywhere."

Anthony slanted his brother an enigmatic grin. "I knew you'd want to meet her."

"What a load of crap."

"You want the truth?"

"No. I just want to gossip about your sex life."

"We're not having a sex life."

"Sucks to be you."

Brett didn't know the half of it.

"She seems to like Nadine," said Brett, taking a bite of his burger.

"That's because Nadine keeps feeding her margaritas. Do you think your wife could slow it down a little?"

Brett licked a smear of mayonnaise from his thumb. "It could work in your favor."

"*You* sleep with drunken women, do you?"

"Only Nadine."

"She's your wife."

"What? You think I sleep with other women?"

"My point is, it's hardly the same thing."

"And my point is, some guys need more of an advantage than others."

"You looking for a fight?"

Brett chuckled and leaned back in his lawn chair. "Don't take your frustrations out on me, bro."

"I don't have any frustrations," said Anthony. And he didn't, expect for a nagging, unrequited lust, a possible murderer on the loose and the impending loss of his favorite client.

He downed a healthy swig of his beer.

On the flight over, he'd started having ridiculous thoughts about winning Joan back. After going through an extensive list of agents in his mind, he realized none of them were good enough for her. Not that he was good enough. But he wanted her anyway.

He considered telling Brett the truth. Brett knew women better than Anthony did, and he might have some useful advice for winning Joan back. But the feeling lasted only a split second. Close families were wonderful, but gossip was a natural hazard.

"What?" asked Brett, peering intently at Anthony.

Anthony took another drink. "Nothing."

Brett glanced at Joan, then back at Anthony. "Something's going on here."

"You're delusional."

"Then why are you two a whole yard apart?"

"Because she's talking to your wife."

Brett set his plate down on the grass. "Listen, Anthony—"

"Don't do this."

"You were there for me with Nadine."

Anthony drank again. "Joan's not Nadine. She's a client."

"She's more than a client."

Anthony glared at his brother. "I don't want to talk about it."

"Yeah. You do. You just don't want me to talk about it to anyone else."

That was true enough. And Brett couldn't be trusted to keep anything from Nadine. And given that Nadine was quickly becoming Joan's best friend, Anthony was keeping his mouth firmly shut.

"You had a fight with her," Brett stated.

"She didn't want to do the *Charlie Long* show." There. That wasn't exactly giving away a state secret.

"And you thought she should."

Anthony snorted. "Of course I thought she should. Only a fool would pass up an opportunity like that."

"And Joan's a fool."

"Joan's not a fool." She might be misguided, but she was a brilliant woman.

"So why did you force her to do it your way?"

"I didn't force her."

"But she did, and she's mad."

"She had a choice."

Brett shook his head. "Anthony, Anthony."

"Don't get condescending on me."

Brett stretched his legs out again, gesturing with his beer can. "I'm going to give you a piece of advice based on my five years of marital experience."

"*Do* tell."

"It's your fault. Whatever happened, whatever went sideways, whatever went wrong, it's all your fault. The sooner you accept that, the better."

"I didn't do anything wrong. And she's my client, not my wife."

"She's a woman. Apologize, and get on with it."

Apologize to Joan? Lie, and tell her she was right to squander publicity opportunities? Tell her she could make a successful career by hiding from her fans?

He didn't think so.

"Quit it," barked Brett.

"Quit what?"

"Quit trying to reason this out logically. Apologize now, apologize often."

"I'd be lying."

"You'd be putting your ego on hold."

"I don't have an ego."

Brett tipped back his head and laughed. "Anthony, you are a slave to your ego."

"Get stuffed."

"It's her career."

"It's my job to give her advice."

"How are you going to give her any advice if she's not speaking to you?"

Brett had unknowingly hit the nail on the head. If Anthony was no longer Joan's agent, how could he give her any advice at all? Who knew what kind of illogical choices she'd make without him?

Maybe Brett was right. Maybe he needed to give a little to gain more influence in the end?

That would mean apologizing to Joan. That would mean backing off and letting her go underground again. But at least it might not mean losing her. And Anthony was nearly sick at the thought of losing her.

CHAPTER TWELVE

THE SUN had set. The kids had been put to bed. And Oscar had turned on the lanterns around the deck, giving the backyard a festive glow.

Brett appeared and put his arm around Nadine, and Joan felt an arm go across her back. She turned to see Anthony's smile.

"Hey," she said and smiled back. She was still enjoying her emotion-denying margarita buzz, and she wasn't about to let anything bother her right now.

"I'm sorry," he said into her ear.

"For what?" she asked.

"For everything."

She saw Brett grin in her peripheral vision. *"Everything?"* she asked, not quite believing what she was hearing.

Anthony nodded. "Yeah. All of it."

"Then you're not fired," she said magnanimously, seizing the moment.

Brett jumped in. "She *fired* you?"

Joan put her fingers over her lips and giggled. "You didn't tell them?"

"I didn't tell them."

"Why'd you fire him?" asked Nadine.

Anthony glared at his brother and sister-in-law.

"Our lips are sealed," Nadine vowed, and Brett nodded to signal his concurrence.

Anthony still looked skeptical.

"Sorry," Joan stage-whispered, feeling rather giddy, more from having rehired Anthony than from the margaritas, she realized.

"Are you going to remember any of this in the morning?" he asked.

"Of course." Did she seem that drunk?

Then it occurred to her Anthony didn't know she'd switched to nonalcoholic margaritas a couple of hours back. She decided it might be fun to mess with his head. She faked a hiccup. "Maybe."

Anthony heaved a sigh.

Nadine giggled in delight. She knew Joan was barely tipsy.

Getting in on the act, she elbowed Anthony. "Might be a few other things she won't remember in the morning."

Brett stared at his wife in shock.

Nadine ignored him. "This could be your big chance," she said to Anthony.

Joan winked at Nadine. Then she walked her fingers up Anthony's bare forearm, feeling dangerous and flirty. "Got any ideas, Anthony?"

He brushed her hand away. "Quit fooling around."

"That's not what you said last night."

Nadine guffawed.

While Joan gave Anthony an exaggerated pout, Nadine whispered something to Brett. He grinned.

"Last night?" asked Brett with evident interest.

Joan decided to keep the joke going. "Last night, he said—"

Anthony's hand clapped over her mouth.

She tried to talk, but no words could get through his grip.

"Joan is going to bed now," he informed them.

She tried to tell him she was just joking around, but he turned her smartly toward the house.

She struggled to get free. She couldn't disappear without saying good-night to her hosts. It would be unbelievably rude.

"*Hmmff,*" she said, gesturing toward them.

"Oh no, you don't," said Anthony. He waved to his parents. "Thanks, Mom. We'll see you in the morning. 'Night, Dad."

Joan renewed her effort to get free. *"Hmmffeeff!"*

"Just a few more steps," he said.

Then the kitchen door banged shut behind them, and he took his hand off her mouth.

"Anthony!"

"Careful." He kept a firm hand on her upper arm, almost lifting her off the floor as they made their way down the hallway.

She redoubled her struggle. "I have to say good-night. I have to thank them."

"Oh no, you don't."

"Yes, I do!"

He glared down at her. "And tell them I think you're the sexiest woman alive?"

"I was joking."

"It wasn't funny."

"I mean, I wasn't going to tell Brett and Nadine you said that."

"Sure, you weren't."

"I'm not drunk, Anthony."

He scoffed.

"Seriously."

He turned suddenly, and she stumbled.

"Okay," she admitted. "Maybe just a little tipsy."

"I've been watching you slam back margaritas for four hours."

"You've been watching me?" That made her smile. She'd been watching him, too. All evening, she'd been questioning her motives for firing him.

But she'd rehired him. That was smart.

They started up the stairs.

"You said yes, right?" she asked.

"Yes to what?"

"To being my agent again."

He stopped on the top landing and turned to face her. "Ask me again in the morning."

"I told you, I'm not drunk."

"Then you can hold your liquor a lot better than I can." He pointed to a door. "Mom told me to put you in Brett's old room."

"What about Brett and Nadine?"

"They're in David's room."

"And David?"

"In the rec room, where there's space for their kids. Why are we having this conversation?" He reached past her and pushed open the bedroom door.

Joan walked in, gazing around at football pennants, trophies and rock and roll posters.

"It's like a shrine," she breathed. Then she turned to throw a saucy gaze at Anthony. "Can I see your room?"

He sucked in a tight breath. "Tomorrow."

She glided meaningfully in his direction and pouted. "Not now?"

"Not now."

She sidled up close, making her voice sultry, thinking how wonderful it would be to kiss him all over again. "You afraid of me?"

"Joan."

She walked her fingers up his chest this time. "Tell me you'll be my agent again."

He grabbed her hand. "Stop."

"Tell me, or I'll rescind my offer."

"You're not thinking straight."

She tossed her hair behind her shoulders. "I switched to nonalcoholic margaritas two hours ago."

Anthony stilled. "So…"

"I'm not drunk, Anthony. Okay, tipsy, maybe. But just enough to keep me relaxed. I will remember every second of this tomorrow."

"And you're flirting with me."

"Yes."

"And you're rehiring me."

"Which one of those makes you happier?"

Instead of answering, he kissed her. There was no preamble this time, no tasting, no testing. The kiss went long and deep from the first second, and every fiber in her body swooned from the exquisite sensation.

His hands roamed their way beneath her blouse, pushing aside her flimsy bra to cup her aching breasts. She pressed her nipple into his palm, desperate to get closer. Nothing was going to tear them apart this time.

Laughter sounded from downstairs.

His family.

Oh, no. His *family*.

He reached behind him and shut the door.

"But—"

"It locks," he assured her.

"But, you," she breathed. "Your room. They'll know…"

"Come here." He took her by the hand and led her across Brett's bedroom. There he opened a door to an ensuite bathroom and guided her inside.

"The bathroom?" she asked in surprise. It wasn't exactly her fantasy, but if that was—

"Not in the bathroom."

He whisked her through it to a second door and pushed that one open.

"My room," he said gruffly.

An equally impressive shrine to Anthony opened up before her. While he locked the door, she gazed around at basketball trophies, boxing gloves and ski racing ribbons.

"You ski?" she asked. It seemed like an odd sport for a Texan.

"Tomorrow," he said. Then he grasped both sides of her blouse. "Do you have any idea how long I've wanted to do this?"

She looked down at his tanned hands against the delicate white fabric.

He pulled. The fabric gave way and the buttons popped, scattering over the wooden floor.

She dropped her head back, and he kissed her neck, drawing the delicate skin into the heat of his mouth, surely leaving marks.

Her hands went to his thick hair, and she moaned his name.

He kissed the mounds of her breasts, dampening her lacy bra while his hands roamed down to her bottom and pulled her tight against him.

She struggled with the buttons of his dress shirt, not feeling any patience at all. They'd been here three times now. Twice they'd stopped.

He grabbed the lapels of his own shirt and ripped it off. Then he pushed her blouse from her shoulders, kissing their curves, tasting the tender skin as he dispensed with her bra.

"Hold me close," she whispered, and then they were skin against skin.

"I can't wait," she told him, wriggling in impatience.

"Neither can I." He reached under her skirt and tugged off her panties. Then he dispensed with his slacks and backed her up to the bed.

He smiled. "Never pictured you here." He gently pushed her down on his bedspread, laying her back and flipping up her skirt. "But what a great teenage fantasy."

She grinned at that one, as he followed her down.

His hands trailed over her breasts, while she explored his firm pecs and delineation of his chest. He kissed her. Gently at first, but then with increasing force and passion.

He cradled her face. "My beautiful Joan."

"I'm sorry," she said, remembering all the hurtful things that had passed between them.

He shook his head. "Shhh." His fingertips trailed along her thigh. Higher and higher, until she gasped out loud.

She was close to the edge. He'd barely touched her, and she was already...

"Now," she cried. Her hips arched and her breathing escalated.

He moved on top of her, grasping her hands, entwining her fingers with his, staring straight into her eyes as he entered inch by careful inch.

She watched his irises, sky-blue, as his rhythm started off slow. Then they darkened to turquoise and sweat broke out on his forehead.

Liquid passion poured through her body, igniting her veins, making her skin tingle and her nerve endings cry out for release. The room grew hotter. The scents grew sharper, and Anthony's rough breathing synchronized with her own.

His eyes turned dark as a midnight sky. And shooting stars took flight on the periphery of her vision. He moved faster, his muscles straining against her body. He was as hard as steel inside her. Her thighs tightened, her breathing held, until her whole world exploded in a shower of shooting sparks.

Anthony cried out her name as she floated through a cloud, spiraling round and round, the earth far, far beneath her.

ANTHONY COULDN'T move.

He might never move again.

Which was fine with him.

He could die right here, a happy man.

"Wow," Joan breathed.

"Wow," Anthony returned, gathering her warm body against him, spoon fashion, in his bed.

"We've known each other how long?" she asked.

He chuckled against her hair. "Ten years." He drew a deeper breath. "Believe me, if my fantasies had been more accurate, I never would have kept my hands to myself this long."

She smiled. "You'll have to tell me about those fantasies someday."

"Someday, I'll show them to you."

She stretched, yawning delicately and closing her eyes. "Sounds good."

He toyed with a loop of her hair. "You're going to remember all this in the morning, right?"

Her lips curved into another smile. "Are you kidding? I'm going to remember all this on my death bed."

"We'll do it your way from now on," he said.

"Do what my way?"

"Your career."

She looked up at him and nodded. "Yeah. That's the only way it'll work."

Her reaction wasn't as gracious as he'd expected.

He felt his jaw clamp down on a rebuttal, and he repeated Brett's words inside his head.

"Because I can feel the pull," she said, her tone softening. "And I have to tell you, it scares me."

"The pull?"

"The pull for more publicity, more notoriety, more sales, more fame, more power." Her words sped up. "It goes on and on and gets faster and faster and more and more seductive."

"What exactly scares you?" What did she mean by seductive? Did she hate it? Or did she like it and hate herself for liking it?

She shook her head. "Oh no, you don't."

"Don't what?"

"Don't start debating the merits of my opinion with me."

"I'm only—"

"I mean it, Anthony. It's my opinion and my choice. I won't let you take that away from me."

He stared down at the determination in her eyes. "Okay," he agreed, repeating the mantra of Brett's words. If she fired him again, he couldn't do a thing for her. If he gave way on some fronts, he'd be there to advise her on others.

It was a tactical retreat.

"Who wants to talk business now anyway?" he asked.

"Not me." She curled her small hand into his. "I like your family."

"They like you."

"They said that?"

"Mom didn't give us connecting rooms by accident."

Joan glanced around. "Basketball, huh?"

"In high school," he said. "By college, I wasn't tall enough."

"Is that when you skied?" She shifted and came up on her knees, reaching to the shelf over his headboard to retrieve a downhill trophy.

"Upstate New York and in Canada."

"Were you good?"

"I won, didn't I?"

"Yeah. But it might have been one of those B-level, northwestern, southern quadrant state league things."

He reached for the biggest trophy at the end of the shelf and held it in front of her. "Junior Nationals."

She put back the smaller trophy and took the national one in her hands, smoothing the gold skier as she grinned. "It's a big one," she said with mock reverence.

He whisked it out of her hand. "Oh, give it back."

"Didn't mean to insult you."

"You didn't insult me."

"You seem a little touchy there about your trophies."

He wasn't touchy. Or maybe he was. He just didn't want her to think he was some hick jock. He could compete with the big boys.

"What did you do in college?" he asked.

She scooted back down under the covers, lying in the crook of his arm. "Played the piano."

"Are you any good?" he joked.

"Didn't win the national junior championships, but I once played with Azek Breeze."

"No way."

She nodded. "It was in their early years. But then my mother found out. And, poof, that was the end of that."

He was impressed. "You could have been a rock star."

"Or Azek Breeze could have tanked because they had a lousy piano player."

Anthony shook his head. There wasn't a doubt in his mind that Joan would have succeeded as a musician.

"That was when my parents knew for sure I was trouble," she said.

He ran his fingers through her silky hair. "You're not trouble. Why do you say things like that?"

"Because I'm always embarrassing them."

"Frankly, I think they're the ones who are embarrassing to you."

She twisted her neck to look at him again. "Are you kidding? Nobody's embarrassing in Chanel couture at the opening of a pediatric hospital wing. My parents might be a lot of things, but they're not an embarrassment."

"Joan?"

"Yeah?"

"Let's change the subject."

She nodded.

"You've got a lot of books to autograph tomorrow."

She relaxed in his arms. "I couldn't believe Nadine had read *everything*."

"She couldn't believe I knew you."

Joan chuckled. "It's a bizarre experience having people think you're somehow special."

"You are special."

"You know what I mean. Leila was afraid to ask me to read her book. She wanted a cover quote, of all things."

Anthony stiffened. He didn't particularly like the idea of Leila capitalizing on his relationship with Joan. "You don't have to do that, you know. She should have—"

"Don't be ridiculous. Of course I'll read her book. And I'm sure I'll love it."

"Joan, you can't—"

"What's that? Business comes before family? Did I hear you correctly?"

"They're not your family," he corrected.

"I'll read her book. For what it's worth, I'll give a nice quote."

"Readers will take your recommendation."

She shrugged.

"If you're not—"

"Do *you* like the book?" she asked him.

"Of course I like the book. I wouldn't have represented it if I didn't."

"Then it's a good book, and I'll like it."

"Joan."

"What?"

"Nothing."

She had to start thinking strategically about her career. She couldn't make decisions to suit everyone else around her. But he wasn't about to start that up again, not when she was lying naked in his arms, and he was starting to think about making love with her again.

He kissed the top of her head.

"You know we have to go back," she whispered.

"No, we don't." Indigo was a bad place for Joan right now.

She flipped over onto her stomach and propped her chin on her hands. "We have to look at my research notes."

He shook his head.

"My book," she continued. "The transcripts of the Kane inquest. I'm the one with the best chance of figuring out what's going on."

"It's too dangerous," he said. "Somebody thinks you know something."

"Then they think Samuel knows something, too. The break-ins have focused on his place, not mine." She was silent a moment. "What could he possibly know that would—"

"Stop doing this, Joan."

"Is there something in the transcripts? Was Samuel a witness?"

"I thought you were taking an emotional break?"

"Break's over. The margaritas wore off."

Well, Anthony sure wasn't ready for the break to be over. But he wasn't about to start another argument tonight.

He leaned forward and kissed her on the mouth, reaching for another condom. "Okay."

"Okay?"

He nodded. "But surely you're not planning to leave tonight."

"Of course not."

"Good. Then we've got at least six hours of our break left." He kissed her again.

This time, she kissed him back. "Why are you being so agreeable?"

He put his arms around her and settled her flush against his body. "It's the new me."

"There's no new you."

"Then it's the old me." He slid his palm over the small of her back and down her rear end, kneading into her taut muscles. "Or maybe it's the aroused me."

"*That* I can believe."

"Good." He kissed her deeply, drawing out her tongue, savoring the sweetness of her mouth. "Because even the agreeable me isn't letting you out of this bed before morning."

She slid her arms around his neck. "Guess I could be agreeable on that point, too."

"Finally. Something."

She giggled, then quickly sobered, peppering his mouth with little kisses while her legs twined sensuously with his.

CHAPTER THIRTEEN

HEATHER SAT cross-legged on the floor of Samuel's trashed bedroom, separating shorts from T-shirts from slacks and boxers while the hot sun set far over Bayou Teche. They'd spent the entire day in the kitchen and living room, and the cottage was finally starting to look livable.

"What happened to all your underwear?" she asked, gauging the relative size of the piles in front of her.

Samuel glanced up from where he was gluing one of the dresser drawers back together. "What underwear?"

She pointed to two pairs of black silk boxers. "Maybe we finally figured out what he stole."

"I sleep in those," said Samuel.

Heather glanced around. "So, where's... *Oh.*"

He laughed and went back to work. "Guess they don't do that in Boston either, huh?"

She stood, carrying the T-shirt pile to one of the empty drawers that hadn't been broken. "It's a lot colder up in Boston."

"And the men are a lot more upright."

"They wear suits. Some of them are wool."

"Poor babies."

"There's nothing wimpy about wearing underwear. *I* wear underwear."

"Sometimes."

"Don't start with me."

"Start what?"

"You're still wearing your sling, bucko."

"I can take it off anytime."

She layered the shirts by color order in the bottom of the drawer. "The doctor told you to wait until tomorrow."

"What does he know?"

"You mean just because he took the trouble to attend medical school?"

"It's my arm."

She returned for a pile of western shirts. "And if you want to keep it, you'll do what he says."

"Are you threatening me?"

She turned to give him an incredulous stare. *"No."*

"You're not threatening to take off my arm if I don't obey orders?"

"I'm suggesting you'll get an infection if you don't listen to your medical professional."

"Oh."

She headed toward the dresser. "You're weird."

"Don't put those in the dresser."

She turned.

"They go in the closet."

She gave him a snappy salute. "Yes, sir."

He grinned. "Gotcha."

"Oh, get over yourself." She tried unsuccessfully to fight the shimmer of awareness caused by his smoldering gaze. Angling her path, she opened the door to his closet. The thief had dragged most of the contents from the closet, and now nothing remained but a few stray hangers on the bar and a black...

She peered into a darkened corner shelf.

Hello.

She set down the shirts and slid the old leather case into her hands. "What's this?" She turned to Samuel, holding it out.

"Dad's fiddle."

"May I?" she asked.

"That's right. You play, don't you?"

"I play the violin."

"*Excuse* me."

She felt a twinge of guilt. She hadn't meant to insult his father. "You mind if I take a look?"

"Go ahead."

Heather set the old case on Samuel's bed and flicked open the catches. When she raised the lid, her breath caught in her throat.

She looked closer, running her fingertips along the satiny varnish and the exquisite arching of maple and spruce. The grain was tight and well defined. But it was the scroll that caught her eye and made her catch her breath. She carefully lifted the instrument from the case and looked for the telltale stylized *A.*

Her heart rate tripled. "Samuel?" It was impossible to keep her voice from shaking.

"What's wrong?"

"This is an Ambrogino."

"No, it's a fiddle."

She shook her head. "This is no fiddle. Ambrogino was second only to Stradivarius as a master violin craftsman."

She pivoted to face Samuel. "Do you know where your father got this?"

Samuel's brow furrowed. "Are you insinuating he stole it?"

"Of *course* not. Quit being paranoid. Does your family have money or something?"

"Only what I make."

"Because this is museum quality."

"I think he got it from his dad." There was a faraway look in Samuel's eyes. "It was just what he played on the porch after supper."

Heather looked back down at the magnificent instrument, her fingertips itching. She'd give anything to play it on somebody's porch after supper. "May I?"

Samuel shrugged.

She drew the bow out of the case, found the rosin and tightened the strings. Then she plucked the strings, bringing them into tune. When the violin was ready, she took a very deep breath.

She started with Vivaldi, the rich tones flowing through her like melted honey. Then she moved to Chopin and finally to a Bach sonata.

When the last note died away, Samuel frowned. "It didn't sound like that when Dad played it."

She couldn't help but smile. "He actually played Cajun music on an Ambrogino."

"Well, that sure made you sound like an insufferable snob," said Samuel.

Heather's conscience twigged again. But Cajun music was repetitious, full of simple double-stops and open string drones. It seemed sacrilegious to own an Ambrogino and not play around with intricate shifting and vibrato.

He crossed to the closet, going to the same shelf where she'd found the violin, and pulled out an old, leather-bound book.

He dropped it on the bed in front of her, staring defiantly into her eyes. "Here's what my dad played. I loved his music. Didn't like yours much."

Heather bit guiltily down on her lip. She'd insulted a man's dead father.

Samuel went back to gluing, and she gingerly opened the leather-bound book. It was full of random sheets of paper, some twenty years old, some maybe a hundred years old. It looked to be original music.

She stared at the beats and run-ups on the first pages—fascinating, intriguing and not nearly as simple as she'd imagined.

She went over the top tune in her mind, mentally feeling out the notes, nodding her head to the rhythm and ghosting the fingering until she was sure she had it right. Then she brought the violin to her shoulder, drew her bow and worked her way through the tune.

When she finished, she looked up to see Samuel standing frozen across the room, his expression haunted.

She set down the violin and rushed toward him. "Samuel?"

He blinked away a sheen of tears.

"Oh, Samuel. I'm so sorry." That had been horribly unthinking of her. He probably hadn't heard that music since his father died.

She placed her hand on his arm. His muscles were taut as steel beneath her fingertips.

"Play it again," he said, blinking her into focus. "Will you play it again?"

She felt her own tears well up. "Of course. Of course I will."

"I know it's not your kind of—"

She put her fingers to his lips. "It's beautiful music.

It's wonderful music. I was a fool to think it was un-deserving of an Ambrogino."

He nodded.

"You okay?"

He nodded again, kissing her fingertips one at a time.

She returned to the bed, spread the music in front of her, and went through a selection of the songs. Some were simple and catchy, some were breakneck and rol-licking.

And Samuel danced.

It was incredible to see such a large man shuffle his feet to the beat. He turfed the sling, and she didn't blame him.

She joined with him when she could, moving her body to the simpler tunes that didn't require her con-centration on the written music.

And when the last note from her final song died away, he pulled her into his arms and swung her around.

He kissed her on the mouth, and she quickly replaced the violin in its case so that she could kiss him back properly. She stretched up, tangling her hands in his curly hair, opening her mouth to welcome his tongue.

"You're beautiful," he murmured, running his big hands down her body.

She pulled her T-shirt over her head and stood before him in her lacy bra. "You ain't seen nothing yet."

He reached out to trace his index finger up her stom-ach, dipping under her bra, deftly clicking the front catch so that it dropped away.

"You got that right," he breathed.

She slipped her hands under his T-shirt, reveling in his hot skin, his tense muscles, the gasp of his breath.

His hand closed over her breast, and he kissed the crook of her neck, his tongue flicking out to leave a hot trail along her collarbone to her shoulder. It was nice. A little sweeter and safer than she'd expected, but very nice all the same.

She urged him to remove his own shirt, and they were skin to skin. He kissed her mouth, smoothed her hair, trailed his fingers along her spine, stopping at the waistband of her shorts.

She kissed him more deeply, waiting for his hands to move down, waiting for that swift, intense sensation, when he took her by surprise. He kissed her back, his mouth roaming her face, her cheek, her temple, the tip of her nose. But his hands didn't move.

Finally, he drew gentle circles at the base of her spine, until she squirmed in frustration.

He cupped her face, kissing her eyelids.

She arched her spine, hinting, waiting, hoping.

He kissed her neck, her collarbone, the mound of her breast. His hand was shaking where it bracketed her rib cage. Okay, now they were getting somewhere.

But then he stopped, and went back to her mouth. She drew back. *"Samuel."*

"What?" he asked from between clenched teeth.

"What are you *doing?*"

"What do you think I'm doing?"

"You're treating me like I'm fragile." She peered at him. "You're treating me like I'm…" She pulled out of his arms. "Like I'm your Ambrogino." She launched forward and smacked him on the chest. "I can get that in Boston, bucko."

He grabbed her wrist, and she hit him with the other hand.

He grabbed that, too, pulling her arms apart, forcing her up against him, breathing hard as he stared down into her face.

"Now we're getting somewhere," she said.

"You want it rough?"

"No. Yes. I don't know. How am I supposed to know? But you've been pushing me, teasing me, *promising* me something different for days now."

A slow smile grew on his face. "You're ready to do what you want instead of what's proper?"

"Yes." She was definitely ready for that. She could go back to being proper next week in Boston. For today, she wanted to belt out fiddle tunes and have wild, unbridled sex with Samuel.

He nipped at her neck, moving down toward her breasts, leaving small love bites as he made his way toward her nipple. "You ever been on top?"

Her eyes fluttered shut, and she shivered. "No."

"You ever been tied up?"

Her eyes flew open at that one.

He chuckled. "Okay. Baby steps."

"I don't. I mean. I—"

He tugged her shorts down in one decisive motion. "I'm not tying you up."

"Good." She licked her lips. It might not be that bad. Maybe...

"You scare the hell out of me, you know that?"

"Why?"

He answered her with rough kisses. "Because you are the most gorgeous, exotic, erotic, repressed... You make me want to teach you everything."

"So teach me."

"We don't have that kind of time." He retrieved a condom from his pocket then shucked off his pants and sheathed himself.

He slid his hands behind her thighs and easily lifted her from the ground. Then he wrapped her legs around him and pulled her into the cradle of his body, immediately sliding inside her, making her groan with pleasure.

He took the few steps to put her back against the cool wall. Then he pinioned her hands against it, forcing pulses of sensation through her body.

"Fast or slow," he rasped.

"I can get slow back in Boston."

He immediately jerked into motion. "That's my girl."

His kisses were soft. The wall was hard. And his body possessed an inexhaustible supply of strength and stamina. She lost track of time and space as fireworks went off inside her head over and over again.

Finally, when she was limp and tingling and totally satisfied, he slowed, then stilled against her. She blinked her eyes open, and the world shimmered back into focus—the plump, white pillows, the messy floor, and his father's violin surrounded by sheet after sheet of priceless music.

JOAN SMACKED a file folder down on the table in the breakfast nook of La Petite Maison. "I just don't get it. What are they scared of?"

Anthony empathized with her frustration. He'd read the entire transcript from the inquest, and he couldn't make any kind of an incriminating connection with *Bayou Betrayal*.

Heather sat up, cross-legged on the window seat overlooking the back lawn and the oak grove. "What do we know for sure?"

"That my parents were murdered," said Samuel.

"That's beginning to look more and more likely," Anthony agreed. He was surprised the state police hadn't followed up on the blunt force trauma suffered by Samuel's mother.

"But why come back now?" asked Joan, picking up Luc's copy of her book. "What is *in* here that's got him spooked?"

Anthony stood up and paced across the room. "And why your parents?" he asked. "Was it random? Was it theft? Did they see something? Were they—" He snapped his fingers, freezing in place. "Is there any chance your parents witnessed a crime?"

"In Indigo?" asked Joan.

"Why not in Indigo?" He turned to Samuel. "Can you remember anything about that week? Did they seem spooked? Upset? Did they try to contact anybody?"

Samuel shook his head. "Everything was normal. It was a Monday. They'd been down to the shack over the weekend. I stayed home because of—"

"The shack?"

"Dad liked crayfish. He had a little shack about thirty miles up the bayou."

"What else is up there?"

"Nothing, as far as I can remember. I haven't been back since."

"Moonshine? Drugs? Gunrunners?"

Samuel frowned. "Moonshine's hardly worth getting shot over."

"Survivalists?" asked Heather.

"Or lunatics," said Samuel. "There's a few people in the backwoods that I wouldn't want to meet on a dark night."

Joan shook her head. "A crazy hillbilly isn't going to follow them all the way back to town and shoot them."

"Drugs, then," said Heather.

It was a distinct possibility.

"But why did my book spook them?" asked Joan. "There were no drugs in my book."

"But there is money," said Anthony. "Or maybe it was as simple as you guessing it was a murder and not a suicide."

"So what are they looking for in Samuel's house?"

"Son of a bitch," Samuel barked.

All three heads turned his way.

"The first time the guy broke in, he went through my photo albums."

Anthony turned cold. "Your parents took pictures that day?"

Samuel shook his head. "No, they were just family photos."

Heather uncurled her legs and swung them over the edge of the bench. "But the bad guys might *think* you have pictures."

Anthony met Samuel's gaze. "Thirty miles up the bayou, you say?"

"Luc!" called Samuel, rolling to his feet. "We're gonna need a boat."

ANTHONY FOLLOWED Samuel's hand signals from the bow, maneuvering the airboat toward an aging dock on the lush shore as the atmosphere and insects thickened around them. They were ten miles down Bayou Teche, another twenty miles into an increasingly complex web of narrow, winding channels that formed tributaries draining into the bayou. The oak canopy had closed over them. Gnarled roots from half-submerged cypress trees twisted between strands of hanging moss that curtained the forest and undulated in a snaking breeze.

If something happened to Samuel, they could be lost out here for months.

Anthony cut the engine, and the big fan blades whirred to silence as they drifted the last few feet. The bushes creaked and groaned with unseen secrets, while insects whirred and chirped in the undergrowth. With a rope in one hand, Samuel grabbed a pillar on the dock and levered himself onto the weathered planks.

"Hold still," he warned the women as he tied off.

Anthony stripped off his life jacket and tossed the coiled stern rope into Samuel's waiting hands. As the craft stabilized, he stood up to help Joan and Heather.

"Spooky," Heather remarked, gazing around at the dense bush as she got her footing on the dock.

"You sure this is the place?" Joan asked Samuel when he handed her up. Anthony released his stabilizing hold on her hips.

Samuel's gaze moved to a narrow, crumbling set of stairs cut into the bank between two sentinel oaks. He nodded. "This is the place."

"So now what?" asked Heather, dusting off the back of her lightweight green slacks.

Anthony hopped out of the boat, automatically testing the strength of the boards as he moved. "Now we check out the neighborhood."

There could be a grow operation or a drug cache of some kind, maybe even a hidden safe house. He didn't want to speculate about shallow graves. Although he imagined the forest would have swallowed up anything like that over the past twenty years.

Joan glanced down at her open-toed sandals. "We're going trekking."

"You two can wait in the shack," said Samuel. "Or out here, if you want."

Anthony moved toward the stairs to see if the Kanes' shack was still standing. There were walls and a roof, at least, although the porch sagged to one side of the small, square plywood building.

Heather smacked a mosquito on her bare arm. "I vote for the shack."

"Let's go check it out." Anthony started up the stairs.

The wind freshened as he climbed, easing the number of insects buzzing around his head. He was too proud to bat at them the way the women were doing. As long as Samuel remained stoic, Anthony would, too.

After a few days in the heat and raw earthiness of Indigo, he was gaining a whole new respect for the residents of Louisiana. The song said if you could make it in New York, you could make it anywhere. He was beginning to think some of these Southerners could kick New York's butt.

They crossed the canted porch and Samuel eased the door open.

It was surprisingly neat inside.

The floor was dusty, but you could see it had originally been sanded and polished. The walls were painted a bright white, and the furniture was protected by dust covers. Whoever last left the shack hadn't been in a hurry. And there were certainly no signs of foul play.

Samuel opened the curtains on two small windows. Then he pulled back one of the dust covers to reveal a willow rocking chair with brightly colored cushions. Next, he uncovered a small, floral couch. There was a dusty kitchen table and three chairs in one corner, and two beds against a back wall.

"Toilet's out the back." He gestured with his thumb.

Heather groaned.

He chuckled at her reaction. "I'll check it for snakes before we leave."

This time, Joan groaned, and Anthony snickered. He wasn't too crazy about an outdoor privy, but he'd be a man about it. "I'll get the water bottles out of the boat."

Luc had thoughtfully provided them with a knapsack stuffed full of drinks and baked goods from the B and B. Smart man. Anthony was already thirsty.

Heather thumbed through a stack of magazines on a side table Samuel had uncovered. *"Good Housekeeping,"* she said, turning to grin at Joan. "Maybe we can learn something useful."

"Speak for yourself," Joan returned. "You're spoiled."

Heather flipped open the magazine. "I suppose that's true enough. I've never used an outhouse."

"It'll teach you a little humility," said Samuel, as Anthony left the shack. Anthony didn't hear Heather's response.

The dock was in full shade now. Between the bent branches of the oak trees, Anthony could see clouds forming above them. He hoped that would bring the temperature down a few degrees. If fall was this hot, he honestly didn't know how people around here survived the heat of summer.

He turned at a series of splashes out in the bayou channel and thought he saw a scaly, green tail disappearing on the far bank. He continued to wonder how anyone survived down here. If the insects didn't get you, the alligators would. And that was before you worried about snakes lurking in the outhouse.

Give him rats and muggers and street gangs any day of the week. At least he knew how to avoid those.

He hopped down into the airboat and grabbed the knapsack from the bench seat. Another breeze came up, and he inhaled the cooler air in relief as he climbed back onto the dock and headed up the stairs.

"You have everything you need?" Samuel was asking the women as Anthony came through the door.

"Anthony." Heather rushed toward him. "My hero."

Samuel snorted. "I cleared the cottonmouth out of the privy."

"I need water before I worry about the outhouse," she retorted. "There's biology at play here."

Anthony grinned. Okay, so Heather could grow on you after a while. He unzipped the pack and handed a water bottle to each of them, then opened his own and drank half of it down.

"So, what else is around here?" he asked Samuel.

Samuel nodded toward the north. "Old Man Barns used to live about a mile up the shore. I'm sure he must be dead by now. And there was a bizarre little hippie place down the other way. Don't remember anyone living there full-time. There's a network of trails out back that'll take us to both."

"Quieter than using the boat?" asked Anthony.

Samuel nodded.

Joan looked at Anthony. "You think there's someone out there now?"

"The guy who broke in the second time pretty much vanished into thin air."

The night photographs Samuel had taken had turned out not too badly, but nobody had seen the man around town.

Joan looked worried. She also looked as if she needed a hug of reassurance. She was obviously holding back because of Heather and Samuel. She and Anthony hadn't announced their new relationship to the world. Not that he knew what their new relationship was, exactly.

He only knew he wanted to hug her, too.

He touched her shoulder, but it was wholly unsatisfying. "We're just going to look around. If we see anything suspicious, we'll report it to the police."

Joan gave a slow, uncertain nod. "Okay."

He turned to Samuel. "You ready?"

"Let's do it."

ANTHONY WAS dripping with sweat by the time they found Old Man Barns's shack. Despite the earlier tease of a wind, the air had stilled and the temperature had crept up several degrees. They found the hippie place easily enough. But it was empty, and had been for some time.

Then they'd circled back farther into the forest, trying to find evidence of human activity. Again, nothing.

They were coming up on the Barns shack along a trail through the bush. There was nothing to indicate humans had used it recently, but then it wasn't completely grown over like some of the old trails Samuel had pointed out.

Suddenly, Samuel put a hand on Anthony's shoulder.

Anthony came to an immediate halt, twisting his head to look at Samuel's expression. Samuel tapped his ear and then pointed to the shack. Anthony cocked his head.

They waited without breathing for a few seconds, and Anthony heard a thump. Somebody was inside the shack.

His heart rate jumped, and his sweat turned cold against his skin. The thump was replaced by a scraping noise, as if something were being dragged across the floor.

Samuel indicated with hand signals that he thought they should approach from the back. Anthony nodded.

They backed into the underbrush and made their way around in a wide circle. Scrapes and scratches formed on Anthony's bug-bitten face and arms. Deep down, he wondered if they were crazy. But he also knew he had to figure out who was threatening Joan.

They made it within ten feet of the back wall of the shack, still camouflaged by the underbrush and the hanging moss.

The noise continued without pause or change. Whoever was inside didn't know he'd been discovered.

Anthony pointed to the right. "Meet at the front door?" he whispered.

Samuel nodded. "Might as well find out if he's armed."

They split up to round the building.

On the way, Anthony checked the small window at

his side of the building, but it was dusty and greasy and impossible to see through.

He carefully rounded the final corner to see Samuel coming the other way. Samuel checked out the front window, then shrugged his broad shoulders. He obviously couldn't see anything, either.

They carefully inched toward the door. It was half-open, sagging on a crumbling jamb. The scuttling inside increased.

Anthony reached out and shoved the door open. Then he and Samuel flattened themselves against the outside wall.

The noise abruptly stopped. But no bullets rang out.

"Hello in the shack," Anthony called, on the off chance it was an innocent tourist or some kind of squatter.

No answer.

"Get yourself out here," Samuel called, more menacingly this time, still crouched low in case whoever it was started shooting.

Still nothing.

Anthony crept a little closer.

Samuel crept a little closer.

Anthony made his way onto the low sagging porch, carefully squinting into the dusty, dim interior, ready to bail if things went wrong. He blinked for a second, thinking he saw bones.

"What?" asked Samuel.

They *were* bones. "What the *hell?*"

Samuel swung up on the porch for a better look.

Suddenly, a massive gator burst full-bore through the doorway, its jaw wide-open.

Anthony shouted a warning, leaping out of the way.

Samuel reacted a split second too late.

The gator moved with lightning speed, its jaw snapping down on Samuel's boot.

CHAPTER FOURTEEN

SAMUEL IMMEDIATELY grabbed a rock and aimed at the gator's head.

Anthony went for its tail, gripping it tight and yelling obscenities at the top of his lungs. He reached for a stick and whacked its leathery skin. "Back here," he yelled. "Back *here!*"

It opened its mouth for the briefest of instants, and Samuel jerked free, rolling over and over, while the gator shot forward, dragging Anthony with it.

"Can you make the tree?" he yelled to Samuel.

Samuel jumped to his feet, limping in a full run toward a huge oak tree.

"Go, go, go!" he yelled back to Anthony as he scrambled up the first few branches.

The gator turned, and Anthony sprinted for a second tree, gripping a branch on the run and yanking his feet up as the gator snapped from below. He grabbed the next branch, and the next one, and the next one. By the time he stopped to look down, he was about thirty feet above the ground, the monstrous gator standing perplexed below him.

"You okay?" he called down to Samuel.

"Not broken," said Samuel. "I'm bleeding a bit." Then he paused. "You sure you're far enough off the ground?"

Anthony chuckled. "Adrenaline."

Samuel laughed and shook his head. "I'll say. I owe you one."

"No problem. You going to be able to get the bleeding stopped?"

"I think so." Samuel had already taken off his T-shirt and was tearing it into strips.

Anthony glanced back down. The gator was gazing around the forest with long, slow blinks. It seemed as though he'd forgotten the near miss. Just another day in the life of an alligator, Anthony supposed.

Breathing deeply, he rested his forehead against the rough trunk of the oak tree. "I miss New York," he griped.

Samuel laughed. "You think this guy developed a taste for Old Man Barns?"

"You see the bones?" asked Anthony.

Samuel nodded as he wrapped a strip of cloth around his ankle. "Looked like they'd been there for a long time. I bet the old guy died of old age."

Anthony agreed. If a gator had killed Old Man Barns, he would probably have dragged him into the bayou. "Seems likely. You going to be able to walk?"

"I think so."

"You're a freaking dangerous man, you know that?"

Samuel chuckled again. "It really doesn't seem to be my week."

"All this and Heather, too."

Samuel straightened on the branch. "Who says I'm involved with Heather?"

Anthony had seen the intimate look that passed between them when they left the shack. "Do I look stupid?"

Samuel considered Anthony's position in the tree. "At the moment? To be perfectly honest…"

Anthony groaned and shook his head.

Thunder rumbled above them.

He looked up to see that the clouds had thickened and closed in. The temperature dropped, and a few fat raindrops landed on the leaves around them.

"This just gets better and better," said Samuel.

"I think you're a jinx."

"Are you kidding? I've survived a shooting and an alligator attack. What have you done lately?"

Good question. What *had* Anthony done lately?

A lightning bolt crackled above them, and he wondered if it was meant to punctuate Samuel's question.

"Well?" Samuel prompted as the rain grew harder.

"I convinced a certain bestselling author not to fire me," Anthony offered.

"Joan tried to fire you?"

"Oh, yeah."

"Why?"

"Because I booked her on *Charlie Long Live*."

Samuel nodded. "I think Heather wanted to fire you for that one, too."

The light was fading, and Anthony had to squint to see Samuel. "You sure you're okay?"

Samuel took a deep breath. "I'm hurt, but I'll live." Then he nodded toward the ground. "Look."

Apparently gators weren't wild about lightning storms, either. While the two men watched, the gator turned tail and ambled down the bank, slipping silently into the rain-speckled bayou.

Anthony would have been lying if he didn't admit climbing down to the ground again made him jumpy.

But he needed to get back to Joan. And they needed to take a close look at Samuel's ankle. And they needed to look somewhere else for clues.

BY THE TIME the last of the daylight faded, Joan was a jumping mass of nerves. The lightning provided sporadic flashes, but that just made things worse. The wind whipped at the hanging moss, creating fleeting, ghostly images that made the atmosphere even more eerie.

"Where *are* they?" Heather's disembodied voice asked from the other end of the couch.

Joan was beginning to worry something had gone terribly wrong. What if they'd found the murderer? What if he'd killed both men? What if he was on his way to the shack right now?

Something bumped against the door, and she let out a squeal of fear. Heather launched herself from the other end of the couch to press up against Joan, gripping her arm tight.

The door opened, and a lightning flash illuminated Anthony's face. Joan could have wept with relief.

But then another flash illuminated Samuel, leaning heavily on Anthony.

She jumped to her feet. "What happened?"

"Why didn't you light the lamps?" asked Samuel.

"What lamps?" asked Heather, the creak of the couch indicating she'd stood. "Where *were* you?"

"Ran into an alligator," said Anthony through the darkness.

The lightning flashed again, and he quickly sat Samuel down in a chair before they were plunged into total darkness all over again.

"Matches are over the stove," Samuel wheezed. "Oil lamp on the windowsill."

Joan could hear Anthony feeling his way across the room.

"You're hurt again," Heather whimpered, brushing Joan's shoulder as she made her way toward Samuel.

Anthony struck a match, and Joan instantly felt better. He put it to the wick of a hurricane lamp, and light filled the little shack.

"There's another on the front window," said Samuel, and Anthony took care of it.

"Let me look," said Heather.

"I'll get one of the water bottles," said Joan, somewhat surprised that Heather was offering to play nursemaid. Her sister didn't have the strongest stomach in the world, and an alligator bite might be pretty horrific.

She prayed that it wasn't serious and took comfort in the fact that Samuel was conscious and at least walking with help.

Water bottle in hand, she brushed past Anthony. "You okay?"

"I'm fine," he assured her. "I got the tail end. Samuel got stuck with the head."

"What *happened?*"

"There was a gator hiding in Old Man Barns's shack," said Samuel. "We scared him up."

"I thought you were just going to look around?" Joan peered into Anthony's face, the yellow light flickering off its planes and angles.

He was the rugged Anthony once again, sweaty, streaked with dirt and scratches. The feelings she'd had in her living room the first night of the intruder rushed back. She wanted him. Right here, right now.

He leaned down and whispered in her ear. "Don't look at me like that."

Joan quickly neutralized her expression and took the new water bottle to Heather.

Her sister looked up worriedly from Samuel's leg.

Joan commandeered the second oil lamp, moving it to the floor for a better view. The cuts were deep and jagged.

"I'll try to find a clean bandage," said Anthony. He peeled back the dust cover on one of the beds, unzipped the knapsack and dumped everything out.

They had water bottles, beignets, cinnamon rolls and a half bottle of French wine.

"Luc runs a classy outfit," said Samuel.

Anthony checked the side pockets and found some cloth napkins.

"Those will do it," said Joan. She turned to Samuel. "You want to drink a little of the Médoc before we pour it on the wound?"

"Hell, yes," he said.

Heather blinked and turned away.

Anthony crouched down beside Joan. "How does it look?"

"Wish I had more medical training," she said. Quite frankly, it looked terrible. But she wasn't about to say that out loud.

"You've had medical training?" asked Anthony.

"No. I said I wish I had."

Samuel chuckled above them.

A sob escaped from Heather.

"Hey." Samuel's voice was soft. "Come here." He held out his hand to her. "It's not that bad."

"It *is* that bad," she sobbed. "I don't know how you can joke about it."

"If I can joke about it, then it can't be that bad." He motioned with his hand.

"I'm certified in first aid," said Anthony.

"Really?" asked Joan.

"Really," said Anthony, and she quickly moved out of the way.

"It looks worse than it is," he said to Heather.

Samuel nodded his agreement.

"It's got to hurt like hell," said Anthony. "But that old boy didn't cut anything vital."

Heather took a couple of hesitant steps toward Samuel. He wrapped his big arm around her and pulled her against him.

"I need you—" he said.

Joan blinked at the pair in amazement.

"—to hold my hand while they pour on the wine," Samuel continued. "That part *will* hurt like hell."

Heather gave a hesitant smile, and the intimate moment was over, making Joan wonder if she'd imagined the whole thing.

"WE HAVE TO STOP meeting like this," said Samuel from the narrow bed in the clinic's surgery room.

Heather smiled as she stroked her fingertips across his forehead, hoping she was being of some comfort. She suspected the codeine and Novocain the doctor had administered were giving him a lot more comfort than she could.

Back at the bayou shack, they'd lain side by side all night long in one of the little beds, listening to the storm crash above them. Samuel hadn't slept much. He'd tried to stay still, but his muscles were tense and his breathing mostly shallow.

"You have to promise me you'll stop taking chances," she said.

"You're holding me responsible for the behavior of an alligator?"

"I'm holding you responsible for disturbing said alligator."

"I don't see how that's fair."

"Who said anything about fair, bucko? I'm trying to have a wild sex fling with you, and you keep messing up your body."

He chuckled at that. "Lie down beside me."

"Here?" She glanced around. They were alone in the room, but the nurse or the doctor could walk in any minute.

"What? No discovery fetish?"

She frowned. "Now that's just creepy."

"Strike that one off the list."

"Definitely."

He reached for her hand, gently kissing her palm. "I'm just messing with you. I want to ask you something."

He shifted to one side. "But it's gonna be a letdown if you were expecting a proposition."

She grinned and lay down on the bed beside him, absorbing the heat and strength of his body. "This is no time for propositions."

He put his arm around her and cradled her on his shoulder. "I was wondering." He paused. "You planning to be in town for a while?"

Heather shrugged. She hadn't given it that much thought. She should have gone back to Boston days ago, but she couldn't seem to tear herself away.

It was nice to see Joan, of course. And she'd pretty

much given up on Paris. For better or worse, Anthony was a big influence on Joan's life. Heather hadn't quite figured out how far it went, but she was kidding herself if she thought she'd get Joan to leave him.

Plus there was the murder mystery. And then there was Samuel. She'd only been with Samuel a few days. She knew deep down in her heart it wasn't enough.

His fingertips stroked her hair. Despite the circumstances and the location, she felt her body respond to the touch.

"See, thing is…" he said.

She tilted her head to look at him.

"If you were to stay for the music festival…"

"Isn't that still a few weeks away?"

He nodded. "I thought… I'd appreciate it if you'd play my dad's fiddle."

Heather turned and rose up on her elbow, her chest tightening with emotion. She was unbelievably touched by the request. "You want me to stay here? For a few more *weeks?* And play your dad's music at the festival?"

"Or you could come back for it." He shrugged, his focus going to the far wall. "Either would be great."

Either *would* be great. But staying would be greater. Staying here in Indigo with Samuel for weeks, and then introducing the Ambrogino to the world along with his father's music.

"Yes," she said in a rush, meeting his gaze. "Yes, I'll play. Yes, I'll stay."

His face lit up with a broad smile, and he eased her down to gently kiss her lips.

Even that insubstantial touch left her breathless.

"But you're going to have to tell me," she breathed.

"Tell you what?"

"When this thing we've got going is over. You're going to have to tell me. Otherwise, I might hang around for a very, very long time."

He kissed her again. Longer, deeper, wrapping his arms around her and holding on as if he were never going to let go. It might have been the effects of the codeine, or it might have been some deep emotion.

"Okay by me," he finally whispered, his voice thick.

AT SAMUEL'S kitchen table, Joan flipped the final page of the final photo album that she and Heather had located in his closets. There were pictures of Samuel at all ages, pictures of his mother, pictures of his father, and pictures of many younger versions of Indigo residents that she recognized.

The older pictures were all from his mother's family. Some were captioned, showing that they'd emigrated from Mississippi in the early 1900s to settle in Indigo. Other members of her family had then left the town in the Sixties, but Maisie had stayed to marry John Kane. Samuel was their only son.

There were almost no pictures of John as a child, and nothing that showed any members of his family.

"Has Samuel told you much about his father's family?" she asked Heather.

Heather turned from where she was replacing framed photos on the fireplace hearth. She shook her head. "No. And it's weird."

"Weird how?"

Heather glanced guiltily around the cottage. They were alone while Anthony picked Samuel up from the clinic.

"You have to promise not to tell anyone," she said.

Joan stood up. "Tell them what? You know something?"

"Not about the murder," said Heather, heading for the stairs. "But, quick, come and look."

She led Joan up the staircase to Samuel's bedroom. There, she glanced out the window, then crossed to the closet and took out an old violin case.

She set it on the bed and flipped the catches.

"I don't understand," said Joan.

"It belonged to Samuel's father. He used to play it on the porch."

Joan stared down at the instrument. It was richly grained and beautifully arched, obviously of very fine quality.

"It's an Ambrogino," said Heather in a hushed voice. "And I played it."

Joan glanced up to see Heather's eyes shinning with excitement. "You think there was money in his father's past?"

Heather shook her head. "Samuel doesn't know. He just remembers his father playing it on the porch."

"This is an incredibly fine heirloom." Joan ran her fingers over the classic varnish.

Heather nodded her agreement. "And that's not all." She crossed to the closet again and came back with a leather-bound book. "His dad wrote music. Cajun tunes."

She set the book down next to the case and carefully opened the cover.

The aging paper was impressive, and Joan's piano training allowed her to read the music. The songs themselves were catchy, but unremarkable.

Joan looked through the pages, picking the fragile paper up by the corners and turning it face down. There was song after song.

"Somebody should copy these," she mused.

"I'm going to suggest it to Samuel." There was something in Heather's tone, a repressed excitement.

"What?" asked Joan.

"Nothing," said Heather. But it was obvious from her expression that it was something.

"What else do you know?"

Heather shook her head.

Joan squinted at her for a minute, then glanced back down at the book. She turned another page and an old black-and-white photograph dropped out.

She picked it up by the white bordered edge. "What's this?"

Heather moved closer. "I don't know. I didn't see it before."

Joan squinted in the light at a man holding a baby boy. They were in what was obviously an opulent parlor in, maybe, 1950. The man was white, the child either black or of a mixed heritage.

She flipped the photograph over. *Gerard and John.*

Joan looked at the front again. John's father? He was white and wealthy and named Gerard?

She peered more closely at the picture, and her stomach felt hollow. "Wow. Oh, wow."

"What?" asked Heather.

"That's Gerard Dinose." Joan's mind scrambled to work out the significance of John's parentage. Gerard Dinose must have had an affair with John's mother, Samuel's grandmother.

"Who's Gerard Dinose?" asked Heather.

"The Dinose family owns half the businesses in Lafayette. They started out smuggling rum, then turned
to sugarcane—"

"Impressive history lesson," an unfamiliar male
voice drawled.

Joan whirled to see a fiftyish, gray-haired man
standing in the bedroom doorway and holding a gun.

CHAPTER FIFTEEN

HEATHER GRABBED Joan, and Joan automatically put an arm around her sister.

"What do you want?" Joan rasped.

The man sauntered forward. "See, that's a tough one now."

Heather tried to back away, but Joan held her ground. She watched the man closely, a weird sense of recognition coming over her. Had they met before?

"You want the violin?" she asked.

The man laughed harshly. "Yeah, right. I went to all this trouble over a stupid violin."

Heather's body jerked in reaction, but Joan held her still.

"Who—" Joan's eyes widened, and her entire body went cold. She glanced at the picture and blinked in disbelief. The spitting image of Gerard Dinose was standing right in front of her.

"Nash Dinose, actually," the man said. "My father's been dead for years."

Nash was John's half brother? That meant he was Samuel's uncle.

So why was he holding a gun on them?

"You're not getting it yet, are you?"

Joan shook her head.

He snapped the fingers of his free hand. "Not clicking in?"

Had he murdered his half brother?

"I suppose I could just shoot you," he mused.

Heather gasped, and Joan's gaze zeroed in on the gun. Should she rush him? Would that give Heather a chance to get away?

"I'm not a monster," said Nash. "But I am a businessman, and I will protect my interests."

"You *killed* them," Heather rasped. She shook free of Joan's grasp.

"Heather, don't!" Joan grabbed her by the arm.

"Of course I killed them," Nash said easily. "I had to kill them."

And Joan understood at last. John must have known who his father was. He was a threat to Nash's inheritance. "They came after your money."

"They might have. And by then it would be too late." His eyes narrowed. "Used to be no court in the land would have recognized that bastard as an heir. But then we got all progressive." Nash's face twisted into a sneer. "I couldn't take the chance."

Joan finished the scenario, her stomach cramping in horror. "So you killed them both and framed John."

"Case closed," said Nash. "Until you came along."

She had absolutely no interest in the sordid details, but she knew their best chance was to keep him talking. "And you didn't know if I knew."

"And you didn't. Ironic. But now you do." His gaze darted to Heather and back again. "You both do."

"We couldn't prove anything," said Joan a little desperately. "Here." She held out the picture. "Take it. Nobody wants your money."

He snorted. "I just confessed murder to you. You think I'm stupid?" He raised the gun and tightened his finger on the trigger. "Sorry, girls. Think I'll frame Samuel for this one."

Joan launched herself in front of Heather.

The shot rang out, but she didn't feel any pain. She didn't feel anything, except a slow-motion descent to the bedroom floor, where Heather cushioned her fall.

She blinked up at Nash, curling her body around her sister, bracing herself for the second shot. There was no way he'd miss twice.

But Anthony was there, one arm clamped tight around Nash's neck, the other struggling to get the gun out of his hand.

A second shot rang out, and Samuel shouted something.

The gun clattered to the floor, and the two men quickly subdued Nash.

"Nine-one-one," Heather rasped in her ear. But Joan's limbs were filled with a strange lethargy, and she couldn't move.

She heard sirens.

She heard Heather call her name.

Then she heard the clatter of boots, and Anthony was standing over her, pulling her into his arms, cradling her head against his chest, kissing her hair over and over again.

"You okay, sweetheart?" His hands moved over her body, testing for wounds.

The world started coming back into focus. Sounds made sense, and things seemed to return to the right speed.

She nodded. "I don't think I'm hurt."

"You sure? Did you hit your head?"

"I don't think so." Her limbs felt shaky, but she was pretty sure it was just shock.

Anthony helped her to her feet.

Alain had handcuffed Nash and was leading him out of the room. Red lights flashed through the window, and Heather stood in the corner, wrapped in Samuel's arms.

"Something's going on between those two," Joan said to Anthony.

Anthony grinned. "You think?"

She looked up at him. "You know something I don't?"

"Just what I've seen."

Joan watched her sister for another moment.

Samuel stroked her face, shook his head, then pulled her tight against him, closing his eyes as if he wanted to absorb her.

Joan glanced away, focusing her attention on Anthony and his strength as he held her. They'd nearly been killed. It didn't seem real, but they'd nearly died.

"Thank you," she whispered.

He chuckled softly. "Anytime, sweetheart."

As her shaking subsided, she was filled with a huge sense of relief. "It's over. It's actually over."

"Almost. There are reporters out on the front lawn."

"Of course there are," she said with a laughing sigh. The sirens would have attracted every reporter in town. And she knew there were quite a few here to cover her story. "I'll make sure I mention the music festival."

"Joan, you don't have to—"

"You think they'll leave if we hide inside for a while?"

He shook his head.

"Then we might as well get it over with. Samuel?"

He looked up from hugging Heather.

"Should we get this over with?"

He gave Heather one last squeeze, then grinned at Joan. "I'm not scared if you're not."

Joan disentangled herself from Anthony. "Like you're scared of anything."

Samuel limped toward the door. "Anthony was the one that brought down Dinose."

Anthony tucked Joan's hand into the crook of his arm. "Only because you're recovering from gator bite."

"This is true," Samuel said to Heather. "Normally, I'm pretty much invincible."

"Thank goodness for that," said Heather. "Otherwise, your stupidity would have gotten you killed a long time ago."

Alain reappeared. "I'm going to need statements from all of you. Can you meet me down at the station?"

"We're going to appease the reporters for a minute," Anthony said. "Get them out of your hair."

Alain nodded. "Don't take too long."

Joan headed down the stairs with Anthony at her side. The minute they were through the front door, six microphones were shoved in her face.

She took a breath. She could do this. It was just like Charlie Long, only with more questions.

"Who was shot?" came the first question.

"Was anybody killed?"

"How does your book fit into this?"

ANTHONY WATCHED from the sidelines while Joan stood on the front lawn patiently answering the reporters' questions. There were three news trucks, at least eight reporters, several cameramen and a multitude of other people running around with clipboards, headsets and toting thick wire feeds.

Amidst the chaos, Joan was doing a great job, and he couldn't be prouder. He didn't think he'd ever get over the sight of her with Nash's gun pointed at her head. If he'd been one minute later, one second later...

He shuddered now just thinking about it.

"Does this exonerate your father?" a reporter shouted to Samuel.

Samuel stepped up, and Heather jostled Joan's elbow, holding up her cell phone.

"It's Mom," Anthony overheard Heather say.

Joan took the phone and backed away from the reporters. His attention stayed with her.

She listened for a minute, the animation slowly leaving her expression.

Anthony cursed under his breath.

"But, I don't—" she started.

Then a silence.

"Mom—"

She heaved a heavy sigh, wiping her damp hair back from her forehead. "Mom—"

Another silence. Her shoulders slumped, and she closed her eyes.

Anthony watched the fight and self-confidence drain right out of her.

She opened her eyes and glanced furtively at the reporters, then she shrank farther into the alcove of the front door.

He wanted to grab the damn phone and pull her into his arms.

"See, I didn't—" she tried again.

"Just—"

Her face went pale, and she blinked rapidly.

Anger welled up inside him. He knew it was her family, but damn it, nobody had a right to crush her spirit like this.

Joan's voice cracked. *"Please, Mom—"*

Finally, Anthony couldn't stand it any more. He'd stood back and watched while these people ripped Joan to shreds under the guise of loving her. This had gone beyond ruining her career. They were totally demoralizing her.

A red haze formed in front of his eyes, and he strode forward and plucked the phone from her hands.

He stuffed it against his own ear. "Mrs. Bateman?"

Joan grabbed for it, but he turned away, holding her off with his other arm.

"To whom am I speaking?" The voice on the phone sounded every bit as imperious as he'd expected.

"This is Anthony Verdun."

The police, the reporters, even Joan herself faded into the background.

"Where's my daughter?"

"She's busy. I'd like to talk to you for a minute."

"Anthony," Joan whispered urgently.

"I *demand* that you put my daughter back on the phone."

"And *I* demand that you stop harassing her."

"Anthony!"

There was a sputtering sound on the other end of the line.

"Further, I demand that you get your head out of your ass—"

"Anthony!"

"—and take a good long look at how much your talented and successful daughter has accomplished. I don't particularly care that your blood's bluer than—"

The phone disappeared from his hands.

He looked up to see Samuel hand it back to Heather.

"You're losing it, buddy," said Samuel.

Anthony glanced over his shoulder, wondering if the reporters had overheard. What he saw was Joan's incensed expression.

Samuel immediately resumed talking to the reporters, raising his voice, walking toward the curb, ensuring their attention was distracted.

"You are *so* fired," Joan rumbled.

"Yeah?" Anthony stepped closer, lowering his voice. "Yeah."

"You think I was rude and out of line?"

"Absolutely," she said without hesitation.

"And you think your parents have the right to speak to you that way?"

Her nostrils flared. "They're my parents."

He shook his head. "Then your biggest problem isn't whether or not I'm your agent."

"Anthony," Heather interrupted.

He held a warning hand up in Heather's direction, keeping his gaze on Joan. He had to say this, and he had to say it now. "Your biggest problem is that you're willing to let them ruin your life. And you know what? I can't stand to stick around and watch it happen."

He turned on his heel.

His head pounded and his gut ached as he walked away. But he'd done everything he possibly could for her, and it was getting both of them nowhere.

He really couldn't stand to watch her parents rip her joy, her confidence, her career out of her grasp. And there was no way he could stand to watch her crawl back into her shell, afraid to be who she was, afraid to love what she loved, afraid to accomplish the things her talent would allow.

He pulled out his car keys and clicked the unlock button. He'd stop and give Alain his statement, and then he was heading back to New York. Stephen would probably fire him for losing Joan, but he couldn't even bring himself to care.

He had a feeling it would be a long time before he cared about anything again.

As Joan watched Anthony walk away, her entire body went numb.

She felt a tug on her shoulder and realized that Heather was pulling on her arm. She allowed herself to be led into Samuel's front hall.

"You know what?" asked Heather as the door clicked shut on the noise and flashbulbs.

Joan blinked stupidly at her. Anthony had left her. He'd left her for good this time.

"Anthony is right," Heather practically shouted.

Joan jerked herself back to life and stared incredulously at her perfect sister. "He just told our mother to get her head out of her ass."

"Yeah. He did."

"Where's the phone?" Joan glanced frantically around. "Where's Mom? I have to—"

"And our mommy *should* consider pulling her head out of her ass."

"What?" Had Heather lost her mind?

"Do you know what I've been doing for the past few days, Joan? Hmm? Do you?"

Joan had to get her mother back on the phone. She had to explain. She had to fix this.

"I've been having wild sex with Samuel."

That stopped Joan in her tracks.

"Yeah. That's right." Heather stuffed her thumb against her chest. "Me. Stuck-up Heather Bateman has been on her… Okay, never mind the details. My point is, I have spent my entire life doing uptight things with uptight people that I never really liked, all because I let our parents tell me what was right and wrong instead of judging it for myself."

"Wild sex?" Joan blinked, not quite getting past that point in the conversation.

Heather leaned forward, staring directly into Joan's eyes. "Things that would curl Mom's hair. Things that would curl your hair. And I *liked* it."

"With Samuel?" How had Joan missed this? They seemed to be growing close, but…

"And you know what I'm going to do at the music festival?"

"You're staying for the music festival? With Samuel?"

What had happened to her perfect sister? Heather always said and did the right things. She'd never insult their mother. She had always put Joan to shame.

"Yes," said Heather.

"Has Samuel given you something to smoke?"

Her sister cracked a smile. "No. But I'd do pretty much anything he told me."

Joan raised her eyebrows.

"It's a whole big world out there." Heather nodded sagely. "But, back to you."

"No. Back to why you're staying for the music festival."

"Oh. Right. I'm playing fiddle tunes. Out there on the stage for all the world to see. I'm going to use my own name. I'll ask them to put me on the posters. And I'm going to send an invitation to every single one of Mom and Dad's friends." Heather gave a *so there* nod.

Okay. That was going to be bad. Her parents would be having coronaries over Heather's behavior. Still. It was one night, one event, arguably something for charity.

"That's still not as bad as—"

"Loving Anthony?"

Joan froze. "I don't love Anthony."

Heather laughed. "He's been your best friend for ten years. You shared secrets with him that you didn't even share with your family."

"That's because—"

"Because he understands you, the real you. He knows you and he loves you just the way you are. Face it, Joanie, you don't have to pretend with Anthony, and he doesn't have to pretend with you." Her voice softened. "Don't you want that? Don't you want that for the rest of your life? To be you, just *you?*"

Joan swallowed. She drew a breath into her tightening chest. To be with Anthony. To come off the stage at the Charlie Long show and have somebody smile and congratulate her and pull her into his arms.

To have a book launch, a real book launch. To talk to fans, to answer their letters instead of logging on to the unofficial Jules Burrell site under an assumed name. To stop hiding and lying and pretending.

Her eyes teared up, and she blinked furiously.

"Do it, Joanie," Heather commanded. "Anthony's right. You have to take control of your life."

"But Mom and Dad—"

"Will get used to it." Heather reached out and rubbed her arm. "What? They're going to disown both of us?"

Joan shook her head weakly. She didn't suppose her dad would let that happen.

Then she remembered what she'd just done to Anthony. The way she'd behaved. The things she'd said— today and in the past couple of weeks. He must be so tired of her psychotic behavior. Even if he agreed to stay working as her agent, he'd probably remain in New York and restrict their communication to faxes and e-mail. She didn't blame him.

But it didn't mean she didn't owe him an apology, recompense for being so shortsighted and self-centered.

She squared her shoulders. "I'm going out there."

"Good for you." Heather smoothed back her sister's hair and wiped the damp streaks from her cheekbones. "You're gorgeous. Go get 'em."

Joan took a deep breath, excitement buzzing to life in every fiber of her being.

THE TELEVISION was playing at the Indigo police station. Those who weren't occupied with the interrogation of Nash Dinose were clustered around the small set, watching reporters alternate between interviewing Samuel live and segueing to experts for speculation about his parents and Samuel's possible claim to the Dinose fortune.

That part hadn't sunk in with Anthony yet. With Nash in jail, Samuel was the only apparent heir to an industrial empire. He wondered if Samuel was ready to cope with that. Then he realized that a man who could cope with gunshot wounds, alligator bites and Heather Bateman all in the same week probably wouldn't be fazed by multimillion-dollar business decisions.

Joan appeared on the screen, and Anthony's gut contracted. He'd pushed his cruel words to the back of his mind, planning to ask himself later what the hell he had thought he was doing swearing at Joan's mother.

Something inside him had snapped. He didn't care who the Batemans were, or what the consequences might be. He wasn't going to stand back and let anyone treat Joan that way. It didn't matter if it cost him his client, his job or his life.

He stood up from the hard bench, drawn to the television set where she was now talking. Perhaps she was disavowing him, publishing and the entire popular fiction world all at once.

"—by my agent, Anthony Verdun—"

Hello?

"—of Prism Literary Agency."

What the hell was she doing?

"It'll be released in March by Pellegrin Publishing. We're all extremely excited."

She paused for a second, but Anthony couldn't make out the reporter's question.

"I'll do *Charlie Long Live* again any time he asks. It was a wonderful experience."

Another muffled question, while Anthony shook himself, trying to figure out if this was a hallucination of some kind.

"The details haven't been nailed down yet, but I'd say

a book tour is very likely. My schedule's been erratic this summer, trying to make deadlines. But I've got some free time now. I'm sure Anthony will set something up."

Anthony slumped back down on the wooden bench. Had somebody drugged her? Had somebody drugged him?

"Thank you all very much," said Joan. "But I have an—" She paused to listen. "Oh. I think my backlist is on the Pellegrin Publishing Web site, and the unofficial Jules Burrell Web site has loads of information. Thank you," she called as she walked away.

She was perfect. She was better than perfect. If Anthony had to design a time in his life when every single professional hope and dream coalesced into a moment of pure brilliance, this would be it.

And it felt terrible. It felt empty. Because Joan wasn't with him. And because he didn't want her to be his client. He wanted Joan to be his lover, his best friend, his soul mate.

He was in love with Joan. He'd thought he could settle for less from her, but he realized now that was impossible.

SHE COULD finally go home.

Joan should have been a lot happier about that.

She thanked the officer for the ride from the police station. It had taken hours to tie up all the loose ends. But even the thought of her own bed and comfort food couldn't erase the hollow ache that had planted itself in the pit of her stomach.

Heather was with Samuel. They were staying at his cottage tonight, finishing the cleanup and starting work on the fiddle tunes for the music festival. Alain was thrilled about that. Heather Bateman was a world-class violinist. People would come to Indigo to see her alone.

Things had worked out just fine.

Joan sighed as she inserted her key into the new front door lock Anthony had had installed. Things had worked out just fine when you considered her career, Heather's happiness and the success of the music festival. Not so fine when you considered Joan's broken heart.

Her fingers fumbled with the unfamiliar lock as her hands started to shake and stinging tears welled up behind her eyes. Anthony was right. All along, he'd been right. And at any point over the past two weeks, she could have told him so and thrown herself into his arms.

But she was too proud. She was too stubborn. For the sake of pretension and propriety, she'd chased away the only thing that mattered in her life.

Heather was right, too. Their parents would get over it. Joan should have given them the chance to get over it years ago. She should have been honest. She should have held her ground when it came to what she wanted and what she believed in, instead of letting her mother bowl her over.

The stiff lock finally gave way, and she wrestled the door open. Safe inside her house at last, she pushed back against the door, clicking it shut and leaning heavily on its solid weight.

She swallowed a sob.

Anthony was gone.

He was probably on a plane already.

She pressed a shaky hand over her mouth and let the sobs come freely as she slid down to slump on the floor of the entry hall. She wrapped her arms around her knees and buried her face in them.

"Joan?" came a soft voice.

She drew her head back, blinking a pair of charcoal creased slacks into focus.

Anthony crouched down. "Are you hurt?"

"Anthony?" she hiccupped.

"What's wrong?"

She scrubbed her palms over her wet cheeks. "What are you doing here?"

He held out a hand and drew her to her feet. "I saw your interview."

"I'm so sorry."

"Shhh." He pulled her into his arms, rocking her back and forth.

"You're not fired," she mumbled.

"And your mother doesn't have her head in her ass." He kissed her forehead. "I'm sorry right back at you. I never should have said that."

She shook her head. Then she nodded. "Yes. You were right. My parents are going to have to get used to me the way I am."

"I'm sure your parents love you very much."

Joan drew back, touching his rough face, gazing into his deep blue eyes, so very, very happy to see him. "But what are you doing here?"

"I was making cosmopolitans. You want to get drunk?"

She nodded. "Oh, yeah." Maybe once she was drunk she'd have the courage to tell Anthony she loved him.

"Good." Then he drew her into his arms again, holding her tight. "Forget getting drunk," he mumbled against her ear. "You want to make love?"

Joan's entire body shuddered in relief. "Yes. Oh, yes."

He drew back once more, his eyes darkening to midnight. Then he slanted his head and brought his lips down on hers. They were hot and moist, and oh so familiar. She lost track of time and space and reason as his tongue made love to her mouth.

Finally, gasping, they drew apart. He kissed her one last time. "Good. Then since I'm on a roll here, you want to marry me?"

Joan's heart contracted. Her chest tingled, and she was sure she couldn't have heard right. "What did you say?"

"That wasn't quite right." He touched his forehead to hers. "Joan, I love you."

Her tears started anew. "I love you, too."

"In descending order of importance, will you A, marry me. B, make love with me. C, get drunk with me. Because it's been one hell of a day."

"It's been one hell of a week."

"Say yes, Joan."

Her broad smile tightened her cheeks. "Yes. To all of the above."

His arms held her closer. "I saw your interview."

She nodded. "So you said."

"My boss offered me a raise."

"You deserve it."

"And a partnership."

"Really?"

He nodded. "Mmm-hmm."

"So my agent is one of the partners?"

Anthony kissed her tenderly. "Your husband is one of the partners."

She rocked in his arms. "I like the sound of that. Are we moving to New York?"

"I say we keep both places."

Joan smiled and nodded against him.

"And Pellegrin already called. They want to talk about your book tour. Nice one, by the way."

"I thought you'd appreciate that."

"Were you trying to win me back with that interview?"

"Was I that obvious?"

He shook his head. "You were that perfect. We have a lot of work ahead of us, you and me."

"That's the truth. Starting with my parents." She glanced at her watch. "I'm guessing they'll be here in a few hours."

"You talked to them again?"

"No. And that can only mean one thing."

Anthony stroked her hair. "You going to be okay?"

Joan inhaled deeply, a sense of calm descending over her. "I'm going to be just fine. You, on the other hand, might have a little explaining to do to my father."

He cringed.

She laughed. "Becoming my fiancé should mitigate his wrath."

"Stroke of genius on my part."

"Your genius is why I hired you."

"I love you, Joan Bateman."

"I love you, Anthony Verdun."

He hugged her so tight that he lifted her clear off the floor. "My darling. You are about to take my world by storm."

* * * * *

HOTEL MARCHAND
Four sisters.
A family legacy.
And someone is out to destroy it.
A new Harlequin continuity series continues
in April 2007 with
A SECOND CHANCE
by Kara Lennox

BEING HONEST IS EASY...TELLING THE
TRUTH IS HARD

The only person who can keep Luc Carter in the little town of Indigo is Loretta Castille. She's also the reason he has to leave. A single mom and local baker who supplies Luc's B and B, Loretta has had a no-dating policy since discovering the man she married was a criminal. Bending the rules for Luc is a possibility, but not if she finds out he's on probation....

Here's a preview!

"LUC IS HANDSOME, isn't he?" Zara asked.

"That he is." Handsome, and exotically different from all the dark-haired Cajuns who lived in Indigo. He had golden blond hair and twinkling blue eyes and a smile that drove her absolutely wild. He talked differently from anyone she'd ever known, with no hint of a southern or Cajun accent. He'd obviously been raised somewhere else—out west, if Loretta's ear was any good. But he'd lived all over the world, if his casual references to France, Bangkok and Thailand were any indication.

Why he'd chosen to settle in Indigo, Louisiana, was a mystery and the topic of endless speculation. For all his easy charm, Luc didn't reveal much about his past except in very vague terms. The fact that he was Celeste Robichaux's grandson ensured that he was accepted in the town. But that was about all anyone knew for sure of Luc Carter.

Didn't it just figure that after almost nine years without a man in her life, Loretta would get the hots for some exotic out-of-towner with a mysterious past? Just like Jim. He'd been an itinerant farmer, handsome as the devil and brimming with funny stories of his exploits. To Loretta he'd been a romantic vagabond, a gypsy, and she'd embraced the notion of wandering the country, living off the land. At eighteen, she'd found Indigo a dead bore, and what better way to escape than to marry a wandering adventurer?

Living on the road with Jim had been an eye-opener for Loretta, especially when she'd discovered how her husband supplemented his income. He stole things—food, equipment, jewelry, even a car every so often. No appeal from Loretta could convince Jim to stop committing crimes.

Then Zara had come along, and the vagabond lifestyle had lost the little appeal it still held. Loretta had wanted and needed a home.

Roots weren't for Jim. He'd been unable to hold a steady job, unable to stay at home for longer than a week at a time. Next thing Loretta knew, he'd been arrested somewhere in Texas for armed robbery. Shortly after his conviction, he'd become a crime victim himself, stabbed to death in a prison exercise yard.

Loretta had mourned him—or rather, the man she thought she'd married, the funny charmer who was never down, who was always dreaming up their next adventure. But she'd learned some valuable lessons. She no longer had a desire to see the world or be a gypsy. She'd come to appreciate the community she had here in Indigo, especially her wonderful parents, who'd never stopped loving and supporting her even when she'd made such bad decisions.

She also refused to throw in her lot with a man again, any man. Who knew what might lurk beneath the surface of even the most appealing guy? Even Luc Carter.

Especially Luc Carter.

He flirted relentlessly with her, but she suspected he

flirted with every female. She didn't take it seriously, but just in case, she took care to make it clear she wasn't interested.

HOTEL MARCHAND

Four sisters. A family legacy.
And someone is out to destroy it.

A SECOND CHANCE

by
Kara Lennox

The only person who can keep Luc Carter in the little
town of Indigo is Loretta Castille. She's also the reason
he has to leave. A single mom and local baker who supplies
Luc's B and B, Loretta has had a no-dating policy since she
discovered the man she married was a criminal. Bending
the rules for Luc is a possibility, but can she find it in her to
take a chance when she learns the truth about his past?

Available April 2007.

HARLEQUIN® *Romance®*

presents a brand-new trilogy by

PATRICIA THAYER

Rocky Mountain **BRIDES**

Three sisters come home to wed.

In April don't miss

Raising the Rancher's Family,

followed by

The Sheriff's Pregnant Wife,

on sale May 2007,

and

A Mother for the Tycoon's Child,

on sale June 2007.

Romantic
SUSPENSE

*Excitement, danger
and passion guaranteed!*

USA TODAY bestselling author
Marie Ferrarella
is back with the second installment
in her popular miniseries,
*The Doctors Pulaski: Medicine
just got more interesting...*
DIAGNOSIS: DANGER is on sale
April 2007 from Silhouette®
Romantic Suspense (formerly
Silhouette Intimate Moments).

*Look for it wherever
you buy books!*

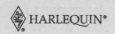

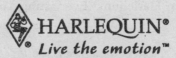